Tw...

orca sports

Anita Daher

Orca Book Publishers

Library and Archives Canada Cataloguing in Publication

Daher, Anita, 1965-
Two foot punch / written by Anita Daher.

(Orca sports)
ISBN 978-1-55143-876-4
I. Title. II. Series.

PS8557.A35T86 2007   jC813'.6   C2007-903165-X

Summary: Nikki blames her brother for their parents' death in a house
fire, but when he gets involved with a gang, Nikki knows she is the
only one who can save him.

First published in the United States, 2007
Library of Congress Control Number: 2007928612

Orca Book Publishers gratefully acknowledges the support for its publishing
programs provided by the following agencies: the Government of Canada
through the Book Publishing Industry Development Program and the
Canada Council for the Arts, and the Province of British Columbia through
the BC Arts Council and the Book Publishing Tax Credit.

Cover design: Teresa Bubela
Cover photography: Charlotte Wiig
Author photo: Sara Daher

Orca Book Publishers
PO Box 5626, Stn. B
Victoria, BC Canada
V8R 6S4

Orca Book Publishers
PO Box 468
Custer, WA USA
98240-0468

www.orcabook.com
Printed and bound in Canada.
Printed on 100% PCW recycled paper.

010 09 08 07 • 4 3 2 1

For my extended family in this dynamic city of Winnipeg, a place that knows when to slumber and when to rock and roll!

Acknowledgments

I offer most earnest thanks to Rob Ray of Renzhe Parkour (www.renzheparkour.com), who willingly answered my questions and read an early draft of the manuscript for technical accuracy; To Liv Rowlands, traceuse extraordinaire, who graciously agreed to let her image grace the cover of this book; To the members of the Winnipeg Parkour team (www.winnipegparkour. com), especially T-mac, who was my e-mail lifeline and team go-between. Hawk, Tom, Kyle, Zeddy, Twizzy, Spade and Riley welcomed me to their first jam of 2007 and answered every question I had left with knowledge, experience, patience and good humor.

Thanks also to Loretta Martin of Center Venture Development Corporation, who took time out of her day to take me through a drippy, dank and fascinating pump station so rich in history; and to Heritage Winnipeg, who put me in touch with Loretta.

Finally, thanks to Jim and the girls for continuing to tolerate and support my writing obsession; to Marie Campbell, the finest, most supportive (and fun) agent a gal could hope for; to all the dear souls at Orca, especially Maureen Colgan, whom I will miss, and Sarah Harvey, my editor. Sarah, you rock! Thanks for pushing me. It has been a gift and a pleasure to work with you again.

Once again I have used real names and nicknames of people I know and have known and pasted them on fictional characters. I do this out of respect.

Within the parkour community there are differing opinions on certain aspects of parkour, free running and tricking. I have tried to use language choices that all will find acceptable. Above all, I have tried to celebrate its philosophy.

Peace.

"It's just being able to overcome anything, to always move forward, to never stop...There's always a different path that you can follow."
—David Belle

"If you can conquer the mind and can open your imagination to all the possibilities the world has, then the physical can come easier."
—Rob Ray

"There's a fine line between parkour and trespassing."

—Hawk

chapter one

It feels like flying.

In the space between where my sneakers leave the concrete and where they hit the top of the next wall, I feel free. One day I, Nikki Louise Stuart, will soar above the rooftops, just like my big brother Derek used to do. But for now these concrete slabs of Winnipeg's River Park Labyrinth are mine. I *own* them.

Unnng!

Okay, maybe not *all* of them. A misstep costs me my perfect landing, but at least I hit the wall square. I wrap my fingers over the edge and scrabble over the top onto the platform. My momentum is good. I roll out and end up head over heels, squatting. Yeah, baby! I smile to myself. After all, there are no real missteps in parkour.

Parkour is about movement. It's about making anything and everything in my path a part of my run. It's about overcoming obstacles by moving over or through them. Parkour is an attitude. Above all it's about being *free*.

At least, that's what Derek used to say.

It's hot, and I've been running hard. My palms feel good pressed against the concrete, which is still early morning cool. The sun is way too bright. If I tip my head forward like I'm praying, my hair blots out the light and gives my eyes a break. Everyone says it's the color of burnt chocolate. My hair, that is. My eyes are blue-gray and kinda smoky, like morning fog.

Standing, I fling my hair from my face and walk to the edge of the platform. It's not the tallest part of the labyrinth, but it's high enough to see all around. When you do parkour, you learn to look at things differently. Better. Your eyes are wide open. Lots of people run in teams, but you don't have to. All you need are sneakers and a good eye.

There's a turret I lean against when I face the river. There are parks to the right of me all the way to The Forks—the place where two rivers join. The Forks is mostly for tourists and shoppers.

To my left and behind me is The Exchange District, full of old buildings made of brick and limestone all decked out with pillars and gargoyles. That's where I live. Right downtown.

This labyrinth is a perfect place to watch people, which is one of my favorite things to do. It's 6:00 AM. All the drug addicts have disappeared, and the tourists haven't yet rolled out of bed. It's early, but I'm not the only one around.

There's Joe Jogger and Jane Jogger, all decked out in matching short-shorts and sweatbands.

And there's Dog Guy. Every morning he walks a bunch of dogs, all sizes and colors, always changing except for one—a Saint Bernard. That's gotta be his own, otherwise how could he stand to stoop and scoop the poop?

My favorite person is Angel—at least that's what I call him. He's an old guy, wrinkled and gray. Probably homeless. I like to think he's my guardian angel. I know he's not, really. It's just something I like to think.

Anyway, he's always on the bench right in front of the labyrinth. I wonder sometimes if Angel even sees me. I mean, I'm always running and doing parkour around here. If he does see me, he pretends he doesn't.

I breathe in one more lungful of morning, and then my belly tells me it's time to go. I run and I run and I keep my speed up as I near a waist-high concrete barrier between a hotel and the road. I plant my left hand first, and swing my bod around in a reverse vault. Skill. That's what that is. There are more places to parkour in the park, but The Exchange has a few hot-spots if you know where to look.

Most of these buildings are old banks. That's why they call it The Exchange—because people used to exchange money for stocks and bonds here. Something like that, anyway. Now it's mostly cafés, shops and upscale loft condos like the one my aunt lives in.

There's a dark side to this place, though. I didn't notice it at first, but it's definitely here—*underneath*. Like biting into a perfect peach and finding the pit split and rotten. I see it in the graffiti. There's the kind street artists do to make some sort of social or political point. I'm cool with that. And then there are the gang tags. Those are what keep me inside at night.

Out of the corner of my eye I catch a shadow moving. It freaks me a little, 'cause I don't expect it. I glide around the corner. Like that's where I always meant to go. I stop. I want to see who else is up this early. Office types are probably still eating breakfast. And it's *way* too early for the usual roundup of creeps. I backtrack to the corner and peek around.

It's a blond guy—short, spiky hair—with an orange T-shirt, skinny black jeans and snake-skin boots. Very cool. He's holding a piece of paper and looking from it to one of the buildings. Checking out an address, maybe...but why now? He looks like a rock star, but I can't see too many rock stars being up at this hour. Maybe he's an unemployed rock star. A *confused* unemployed rock star.

I start around the corner, thinking I might give him directions, but I stop when I see a car roll up beside him. I duck out of sight again. I don't know why. I'm just careful, I guess.

The car is an old Popsicle-green Corvette. The rock star bends toward the driver's window, and then he goes to the passenger side and opens the door. Before he gets in he looks my way. I flatten myself against the building. Like I said, I'm careful.

After a few seconds I look again. No man. No green Corvette. Weird, but whatever. My stomach growls at me to get home. Okay stomach, just chill a sec.

At the corner of my aunt's building I stop and look, just like I always do. There's a plaque engraved with the building's name and the date it was built.

Zloty
1911

I wonder who Zloty was? You have to be someone important to have a whole building named after you. The doorman, Cujo, tips his powder-blue cap as I jog past the front entrance. Having a doorman is cool, but what I do next is way cooler. Around the corner I pick up speed, and then I spring two steps off the wall to get over a gate. In parkour we call those wall-steps a tic-tac. A few more vaults and pull-ups, and I'm on my aunt's balcony on the fourth floor. When I open the door a scream nearly blows my eardrums.

"Chill, Auntie Sylvia!"

"Oh lord, Nikki, I will never get used to you coming in that way." Auntie Sylvia looks a bit pale.

"You're a judge, Auntie Sylvia. You should know the value of a good lock."

Auntie Sylvia grins. She's pretty good at bouncing back. Maybe she'd be good at parkour. "You mean to tell me that if I locked that door you would start coming up like a normal person?"

"Hah! You don't see much 'normal' in downtown Winnipeg, not unless you think hanging out with hookers and junkies is normal." I clamp my mouth shut, but it's too late. We're probably both thinking the same thing.

Auntie Sylvia scrapes scrambled eggs onto two plates and joins me at the table. "Do you know what time your brother got in last night, Nik?"

"No," I lie, "I can't hear much from the back bedroom." Actually, I know exactly what time my brother came in. His key scraped the outside of the lock in the hall for what seemed like forever before he finally fell through the door. He was breathing heavily, and I heard him swear when he fell against the wall. I stared at the ceiling, wishing I was asleep. I didn't want to hear what came next. Puking.

All I know is that my clock was blink-blink-blinking 4:08 AM.

"He's going through a tough time," Auntie Sylvia says.

"So am I!"

"I know, honey, but maybe you're stronger than he is."

Maybe now, but it wasn't always like this. Derek's just two years older than me. Okay, he's eighteen, and I'm *almost* sixteen. When we were in Toronto, he was the best on his parkour team. They were called The Rude Boyz, and Derek went by the nickname Ace.

They all had nicknames. I always wondered what my nickname would be if I were on the team. I was good enough to be on the team. I knew it, Derek knew it and the rest of The Rude Boyz knew it too. But it didn't matter. Whenever I asked if I could join, they laughed at me like I was a little kid. They were rude all right. Man.

At least Derek let me practice with him.

"Why can't I join?" I'd ask him as we ran.

He'd tell me that if it was up to him I could. In a heartbeat. But the other guys wouldn't listen. He said that after I turned sixteen he'd talk to them again.

Being shut down by the team had stung, but Derek always had a way of making me feel like the queen of the world. My brother, best of The Rude Boyz, believed in me.

I believed in him too. But that was before he killed our parents.

chapter two

I don't usually run so late in the day—too hot—but I'm feeling a bit weird. Unsettled. Maybe it's the sirens. I don't like them, even though they've become the soundtrack to my life. City music. Sirens never used to bother me, but there are a lot of them today, and close. I think they're fire sirens, and that makes my heart pound a bit wacko; my breath comes in short little puffs. Like I said. Weird.

When I stand on the balcony and look out I don't see anything, but that isn't unusual.

The buildings in The Exchange are all different sizes and shapes, and sometimes it's hard to see past the angles. Anyway, I hope it isn't a fire. I don't smell anything. Maybe it's a false alarm.

Maybe it isn't the sirens at all. Maybe my aunt is making me jumpy. I can tell she is worried. At breakfast she was about a million miles away. I asked her what was wrong, and she said, "Nothing. Just work."

Auntie Sylvia is a judge. She's the judge on a major criminal case—it's been in all of the newspapers and even on national TV. It has to do with gangs and police corruption. Actually just one bad cop so far—the defendant—but the dude was pretty high up in the ranks. They think there are more guys like him, but so far no one's talking. That's got everyone a bit jumpy. So jumpy that they built a special extra-secure temporary courtroom in an old bank building in The Exchange District.

And then there's Derek. I hardly talk to him anymore, what with his vampire hours, but today I hung around until he got out of bed at 2:17! He never used to sleep that late.

Anyway, he wouldn't talk to me. Ever since we moved here he won't hardly look at me. And it's getting worse.

It always feels better to be moving.

It's fry-an-egg-on-the-sidewalk hot today. I take it easy over the tops of my labyrinth, and jog to the nearby play-park.

Two moms in sun-hats are sitting on a bench, watching their children on the swings and slides. I can see them frowning at me as they slather on another layer of sunblock. Jeez, just because I'm here, doesn't mean I'm here to cause trouble. It's a free park! They stare at me as I do handsprings off a bike stand.

"Are you in a circus?" one of the kids asks me.

The moms aren't comfortable with their kiddies talking to the big bad circus freak, and pretty soon they call their kids back, and they all take off toward the river.

Alone at last! I've had my eye on the gray brick wall on one side of the sandpit. There's something I want to try, and I don't want an audience. Derek always told me there were some moves I shouldn't try until I was sixteen. He said that some of my muscles wouldn't be fully formed until then, and I might get hurt.

Whatever. My sixteenth birthday is next month. I don't want a party—that wouldn't feel right. Auntie Sylvia says maybe we should make a trip back to Toronto instead. She says it's been three months, and it might be good to go back.

I know she's trying to help, but it makes me feel worse. Maybe she needs to say some sort of final good-bye to Mom. I mean, I know they were sisters and all, but what's the point of going back? There's nothing left for us there but bad memories and more tears. I don't talk to my friends there anymore. Not even my best friend, Shanna. When I think of Shanna I think about how normal everything used to be. Hanging out in the mall, going to a movie, midnight glow-bowling. I remember Shanna showing Mom some dance moves. I feel bad now, because I laughed at the way she danced—my mom, not Shanna.

I want to cry again. Forget it. There's no going back.

So, here I am. Just me, a wall and this great move I want to try. For a second I wonder if I can do it, but then I tell myself it's just a back flip done off a wall. I wish Derek was here, but oh well. He'll have to be stunned by my skill some other time.

It's now or whenever, baby. I sprint to the wall and step one, two, three, up.

Oof!

Okay, that didn't go so well. I take a minute to figure out where my wind went. Must have got knocked into this sand.

The sand doesn't smell right, and I wonder if someone peed in it. I toss my thoughts outward. My skin feels tight where the sun is hitting it. Blue sky peppering through fraggle-headed trees. A squirrel chittering.

Hot, hot, hot. I can feel the moisture in the air, though. It's like breathing through velvet. It'll rain before morning—at least, I hope so.

I push myself up and out of the sand. It's time for another go.

Focus.

Derek used to say a person could think too much sometimes. Just do it.

Up the wall—one, two, three, flip—

"Awesome!"

What the...? I land well this time and spin around to see who shouted.

"Do you do gymnastics?"

A girl I don't know is squatting on the back of the bench. Good balance! Her hair is shiny black and cut straight, just above her shoulders. She's got bangs over blue eyes. The way her eyes curve upward just a bit makes me think of a cat. The girl leaps from the bench to the sand.

"It's not gymnastics," I tell her.

"No? What is it? I'm Rain, by the way." The girl's smile is like a hug. I smile back.

"I was training for parkour. That move was a wall-flip."

"It's very nice to meet you," Rain says, still smiling. "What did you say your name was?"

I feel myself flushing. "Sorry—I'm Nikki."

"It's very nice to meet you, Nikki," Rain says again. "Whatever you call this, it's uber-cool. Do it again!"

"I'm not sure I can."

"Try!"

Shrugging, I square myself and run for the wall one more time. Success! It's like I've done this move dozens of times already.

"That totally rocks! Tell me more about— what did you call it?—parkour."

"It's mostly just running, with some other moves thrown in. It's about getting from one place to another by making the stuff in your way a part of your run. You climb and jump things instead of avoiding them."

"How come I never heard of it before?"

I grin and sit on the bench. Mom used to say, *Be careful what you wish for*! I was wishing for rain, and here she is! Not *quite* what I was expecting but kinda nice, anyway.

Rain plants herself cross-legged in the sand and waits for me to explain.

"It's still pretty new," I say. My neck is sweaty, so I lift my hair to let the air get at it. "It started in France a few years back. Some famous runner wanted to make his practice runs more interesting, I think, and used some

17

of his dad's old military moves. My brother knows more about it than I do. He was on a team where we used to live. I don't think there are any teams here, though. I haven't heard of any."

"Then why do it?"

"Why do anything?"

"Yeah...I get that," Rain said. "The reason I asked you if it was gymnastics was because your wall-flip looks like a gymnastics move."

"You do gymnastics?"

"Yeah. Some of the kids at school don't get why I want to push my body instead of abuse it."

"You mean with drugs?"

"Whatever."

I look down the walk to where Angel usually sits. The bench is empty, but maybe he put in a good word for me. Or maybe it was Mom, watching over me, making sure I made a new friend.

There's a lump in my throat, and it hurts. Swallowing doesn't help.

I push through it. "Parkour actually uses some gymnastics moves," I tell her. "Some martial arts too. Want me to show you some-thing?"

"Yeah!" Rain cries, springing to her feet.

"Okay...safety first. You can do a roll, right?"

"Duh!"

"You need to roll out properly so you don't hurt your spine."

"Fine. Teach me something!"

"The first thing my brother showed me was a monkey vault. We can do it over this bench and roll into the sand. Watch."

I run straight for the back of the bench, step my feet together, plant my hands on the bench and punch off the ground. I tuck my feet up, under and through my arms, which I keep straight. On the other side, I land in a crouch, on the balls of my feet. I roll out diagonally from my right shoulder to my left hip and back up onto both feet.

"Interesting," Rain says. "In gymnastics I usually take off from one foot."

"It's called a two foot punch. Want to try?"

Rain nods.

"Okay—follow me."

Hop, two foot punch, vault, over. I roll out just in time to see Rain almost on top of me. I throw myself out of her way. "Hey!"

"—is for horses," Rain finishes, laughing. "Too easy! Show me something else."

I look around. "Okay...I bet you can do this too." I get up, brush the sand off and jog to the wall. I do an easy tac off the wall, planting one foot against bricks, and pushing off.

"No problem," Rain says, following.

"Okay, now try this." I approach the wall again. This time I punch off the ground, plant my hands on the wall and use my momentum to rotate my body by spinning my legs up and over. Rain tries it too. I smile. Not bad for a first try—the girl is a natural!

"That's called a wall-spin," I tell her.

"Cool! Looks like I can do parkour too. Where can I sign up?"

"Guys who do parkour are called tra-ceurs," I tell her. "You would be a traceuse, like me...but there's nothing to sign up for. No teams in Winnipeg, remember?"

"That doesn't mean we can't have some fun. You go, and I'll follow."

I hesitate. I don't like to run when it's so hot, but I wouldn't mind showing her a few moves. "Maybe just a short run. Okay?"

Rain nods, and we begin with a jog around the play-park. We run up and over the bench, swing through the monkey bars and tic-tac across the wall. Now I know Rain can keep up, so I take the path, hopping from guard rail to guardrail. Then it's up the slope to the labyrinth. I run up the outer wall and scrabble over the top. I leap from one wall to the next in a move called a cat-leap and stop only when I reach my favorite platform. The heat has kicked me in the gut, and I'm gulping to catch my breath as I turn, expecting to see Rain right behind me.

I'm alone.

chapter three

"Rain?" I call. Then louder. "Rain, are you there?"

I hear nothing but twitter-birds and muted city music from somewhere up the hill.

"Yah!"

I jump sideways as Rain springs from behind the turret. "How did you...?"

Rain is bent double, laughing. Slapping her knee, she straightens and wipes an eye. "You should have seen your face!"

"I bet," I say. I try to smile, but I'm annoyed. I hate being frightened. "I thought you quit."

"Are you kidding? I didn't quit—I failed. I kept up until you started hopping from wall to wall. You have a name for that move?"

"A cat-leap."

"Okay. Anyway, I fell about three cat-leaps back and figured I'd run through the maze to catch you."

"You caught me all right."

Rain sits down and swings her feet over the edge of the platform. She motions for me to sit too. "Sorry if I scared you. Are you mad?"

"Not really. I guess I'm not big on people jumping out at me."

"Smart woman—you'll do fine around here. Where'd you say you moved from?"

"Toronto."

"Why'd you move?"

I swallow, wondering how much I should say. "My parents died. In a fire."

"Oh..." Rain turns to me, cat eyes full of sadness. "I'm so sorry, Nikki."

I hate seeing that look in Rain's eyes. It's the same expression everyone has when they find out about my parents. They touch my arm and then they back away, as if they're afraid my bad luck will stain them. Or maybe they just don't know what to say. Whatever. I'm blinking back tears. I *so* don't want to cry. Not now.

"Oh, man, I'm such a jerk!" Rain moans. "First I scare you, and then I make you cry. What can I do?" She looks around. "Why is there never a mime around when you need one?"

"A mime?"

"Sure! Anytime you think life really sucks, just imagine a mime and be glad your life doesn't suck like that."

"I like mimes!"

"Oh yeah?" Rain moves her hands like she's trapped inside a glass box. I laugh. The annoyance and the sadness retreat.

"I don't even like to pretend to be trapped like that," Rain says. "It's better to do what you do."

"Parkour."

"Yeah. Can I run with you again some-time?"

I smile. "Sure. I'm here most mornings around six."

"Six? Are you kidding me?"

I shake my head.

Rain sighs. "Okay, six it is. I'll see you tomorrow?"

"Okay."

Rain waves once before she disappears around the bend of the river path. As I rise to leave I feel something odd inside. A lightness. It's been a while. Running on my own has been okay, but I miss having company. I miss running with Derek.

Meh. Those thoughts are pointless. I've got to move on. Maybe hanging out with Rain will help.

I sigh; then I hop from my perch and roll out on the grass below me. I jog back into Winnipeg's heart. Across the old market square park, the buildings offer a small measure of shade. It feels good. Better, anyway. I pick up my pace, run up and over some benches and into an apple tree. It's leafy and grand and a good place to hide when you just want to be left alone to people-watch. There are always interesting-looking people in the square.

To my left, shops are closing up for the day. Pigeons run from a straggling shopper who is overloaded with brightly colored bags. All at once the birds fly up and move together like they're synchronized swimming in the air. An old man, gray and rumpled, shuffles along the walk toward a bench. Angel!

On impulse, I wave. He looks at me, startled, and then turns and plants himself on the bench. Oh well. Guess he's not the sociable type.

In front of a restaurant with a sign shaped like a giant onion, a girl and a guy hold hands as they read the same page of a book.

To my right, people flow in and out of a busy British-style pub.

From the corner of my eye I catch a flash of motion at an old-style parking garage that's shaped kind of like a barn. I'm too late to see more. Whatever it was is gone now, out of sight behind the garage's graffiti-tagged doors. I watch as a man shuffles from around the corner toward the garage. He's wearing a ballcap backward, and he's swaggering like he's some kind of a tough guy. His hands are in the pockets of his baggy, gray, canvas pants.

I can see the other guy now—the one who disappeared into the garage. A head pokes out—a head with toffee-colored curls. Derek! Nice to see him out in daylight. Maybe he's not a vampire after all.

Ballcap guy is talking to him. I frown. What's up with that? Are they friends? It looks like they're up to something. Ballcap guy definitely looks like bad news, and Derek has changed so much since we came here— drinking every night, coming in late. Not the brother I used to have.

As soon as ballcap guy moves off, I'm out of the tree and catching up to Derek.

"What's up, big brother?"

"The price of oil, little sis. What do you want?"

I plant myself in front of him. "What were you doing with that guy?"

"He's a movie director and he wants to make me a star."

"Cut it out, Derek! I'm serious. He looked super-shady."

"Forget it, Nikki. I wasn't doing anything with him—he only wanted directions. Even if I was doing something, it's my business, not yours." He shoves past me and keeps walking. I don't like the clammy look of his skin.

"Did it ever occur to you that what you do *is* my business? You're my brother. Next to Auntie Sylvia, you're the only family I've got."

I think I see a flash of pain in his eyes. He stops walking.

I stop too and wait for him to speak. It looks like he wants to, but he's just staring at the sidewalk. It's almost like he's forgotten I'm here.

"I'm sorry, Nikki." His voice is soft, barely more than a whisper.

"For what...? What are you planning, Derek?"

He shakes his head and exhales. "I'm sorry for everything, Nikki. It's my fault—the fire, Mom and Dad, everything."

I'm so shocked, I open my mouth and nothing comes out. After the fire, we were both devastated—even more after we learned that it had been caused by a cigarette butt left burning in the attached garage. Derek didn't smoke, but a girl he liked did. It was his fault she was there and his fault she'd been smoking in the garage. It was his fault that he hadn't made sure the butt was completely snuffed before throwing it in the garbage can.

Hours later, the smoke alarm had woken me and my parents. We escaped, but when Derek didn't come out, Dad went back in for him. Mom ran in after Dad. They said the fire trucks were taking too long. But Derek wasn't even there. He'd snuck out to be with the girl.

Even though it was his fault, the police and the fire department called it an accident. Even though it was his fault, he hadn't even said he was sorry. Until now.

He wants me to forgive him, but I can't. I can't even tell him I still blame him. Not out loud.

29

That lump is back in my throat, and it hurts. "Mom and Dad are dead, Derek," I say, swallowing. "I don't want to lose you too."

He looks at me, his eyes haunted. Despite the heat, I shiver.

"Maybe you should," he says.

chapter four

There's something about a city's heart that is so beautiful.

I run, breathing in air that's moist and fresh. I was right about the rain. It poured so hard last night it was like someone turned on a pressure washer or ran The Exchange through some monster car wash. It feels like it's going to be a good day.

At the river's edge, I see a lean figure standing in a patch of clover outside the labyrinth, glowing in the morning sun. Rain in the sun. I smile.

"You made it," I say.

"Yeah," Rain says, grinning. "But I was beginning to wonder if you would."

"I'm on time!"

Rain taps her watch. "You're a minute and a half late," she says in a mock school-marmy voice.

I laugh. "Okay, fine. You can give me hell, but only if you can catch me."

With Rain on my heels, I begin with a fast jog. Just past the play-park there is a grassy area lined with thick wooden posts sticking up from the earth. They mark where the play-park begins and the rest of the park takes a break. I begin hopping from one post to another.

"This is called precisioning," I call over my shoulder. "We can do this on ledges and rails or almost anyplace with space to land."

"No problem," Rain says.

Apparently it is a problem. She wipes out on the first post.

"When you jump," I say, "tuck your knees up. And when you land, put your arms behind you for balance. Then push off to the next post."

Rain tries again and soon gets the hang of it. We hop silently in the morning hush, from one post to the other, like some sort of champion leap-frogging team.

"This is hard work!" Rain huffs.

"Harder than it looks," I huff back. "It's important to get it right."

"Good exercise too!" Rain said.

There's a commotion as Dog Guy staggers around the corner, struggling with six leashes. Today he's got a poodle, two basset hounds and two, brown, scraggly dogs with pointed ears and nubs for tails. And of course there is the Saint Bernard. They all shuffle past in a panting mass of legs and fur until they are right in front of the labyrinth. The Saint Bernard stops and squats.

"Ew," Rain says.

"Same thing, every day," I say, laughing. "Don't you like dogs?"

"My next-door neighbor has two giant mutts that are always barking their heads off. I guess I'm more of a hamster or fish person—something quiet and not so gross to clean up after," she says.

We watch as Dog Guy drops the freshly scooped and bagged package into the waste-bin beside the walk.

"Where do you live?" I ask. I guess I figured she lives somewhere downtown, like me. But if her neighbor has big dogs, maybe she lives someplace with yards.

Rain points to the bridge that arches across the river at The Forks. "That way," she says. "Just a few blocks from the river on the other side."

"Huh," I say. "Hard to believe there are suburbs so close to here."

"It's hardly the 'burbs. There are some nice neighborhoods and some not so nice— just like everywhere. My house was built about a hundred years ago."

"Do you have brothers or sisters?"

"Nope. It's just me and my mom," Rain says, shrugging. "Hey, do you want to talk or run?"

"I always want to run!"

Talking can wait. I hop from the post I'm on and hit the path. At the play-park we tic-tac off the brick wall. Along a walkway we jump from rail to rail, practicing our precisions.

"Try this!" Rain shouts, as she punches off a post and somersaults through the air.

"No problem," I say. Okay, small problem. I'm not as graceful as Rain, and I angle my somersault more toward the ground before rolling off my shoulder to standing.

"Not pretty," Rain says, "but I guess it'll do."

"Whatever! Listen to the student teaching the teacher!"

Grinning, we run side by side past the labyrinth and up the hill to the downtown. In an alley, Rain wants to stop.

I look around. There are no real obstacles to play with. Just faded brick buildings. I check out two of them. They're almost back-to-back. About one floor up, old metal staircases climb up their sides. They're close enough that if you stand on a landing and stretch, you can probably grab the staircase on the other side.

"What can you do here?" Rain puffs, out of breath.

I shake my head. "Nothing much. There's a fine line between parkour and trespassing."

"Come on. No one is looking. I dare you."

I glance up and down the alley. "Okay. Why not?"

With a practiced eye, I plan my moves. I sprint to where the buildings are closest and tic-tac from one side to the next. It looks like I'm running up the space in between. As soon as I'm close enough, I leap for a staircase rail and then cat-leap from one side to the other, climbing higher and higher. My arms burn from the effort. Finally, about four floors up, I stop. "That's it," I huff. "No more!"

"Holy, that's impressive! I thought you were going to go all the way."

I squint into the square of blue above me. I'm about halfway up. Not bad. Except for Auntie Sylvia's place—which is totally easy for me—I haven't done much climbing since we left Toronto.

I let myself not-quite-freefall, grasping rails on the way down, finding footholds to match. At the bottom, I collapse. I sit cross-legged, rubbing my shoulders. "Guess I should do some pull-ups," I say. "I need to strengthen up."

"I think we should both do pull-ups," Rain says. She looks up to where I was climbing and then turns to me, eyes bright. "Come to my gym to work out. Then we can come back and I'll try it too!"

I grin. There is something about Rain that makes me feel special, as if I can do something nobody else can. Maybe that's true, especially since Derek's given up on everything, even himself.

"Deal," I say. "You can be my new running partner. Welcome to the wild and wonderful world of parkour."

chapter five

Derek is gripping a mug of foul black stuff that was coffee when it was freshly made. But that was hours ago. He doesn't look like he cares that it's old or cold. Can he even see it? His eyes are bloodshot. Looks like it hurts to blink. He's holding onto that mug like it's going to save his life.

At least he's awake. And it's not even eleven o'clock! Shocker.

"Why are you doing this to yourself?" I ask, squeezing lemon into my tea. It would have been iced tea, except it's cool and damp this morning. Hard to believe two weeks earlier it was so hot. In spite of my annoyance with Derek, I smile to myself. That was when I met Rain.

But Rain has nothing to do with the mood at this table. Neither does the temperature outside. I shiver and zip my hoodie up to the neck.

"I'm not doing anything," Derek grumbles. It looks like he's having difficulty moving his lips, as if every word is an effort. "I'm eighteen. That makes me legal to drink in Manitoba."

"That doesn't mean you should." I sound like a parent. Before I say something I can't take back, I bite my lip and watch as he tips the sugar bowl toward his mug. Too much sugar falls into the black. He stirs the coffee with his finger and then sucks off the sweetness. Uggh. How can he drink that stuff? The idea of it makes my stomach scream.

"It's none of your business, Nikki," Derek says.

"So you keep telling me," I snap. "Except

that's not true, and you know it. What happened to my big brother, the best traceur around? What happened to Ace?"

"Didn't you hear? Ace decided to fold."

"You're sick, Derek, and I don't just mean in the head."

"So what? My business."

"Mine too!"

"Leave me alone."

"Is that what you want, Derek? Really? Auntie Sylvia keeps saying to give you some space. But I'm getting sick of it."

"Auntie Sylvia is right."

"Maybe about some things, but not this. What's the plan, Derek? Are you going to pump your body full of poison until you're dead?"

"So what if I do?"

"You can't! You're my brother..."

"You've got Auntie Sylvia. You don't need me."

"I *do* need you, Derek," I say, pushing my chair back and standing up. "But you're right. I don't need you like this."

With fire in my belly and fists clenched,

I leave him to his sweet sludge. I grab my sneakers from beside the door and slam the condo door shut behind me. Sitting in the stairwell at the end of the hall, I pull the sneakers on and listen for the door of our apartment to open, hoping that Derek will come after me. I also hope he won't.

The door behind me stays closed. Here come the tears. Stupid tears. They're making me blind, but I stumble down the stairs anyway and out through the front entrance. Turning my face away from Cujo, I give him a wave. I don't need to look to know he'll be tipping his cap the way he always does.

Cujo arrived on the scene not long after Derek and I moved in. Auntie Sylvia asked him what happened to the old doorman. Cujo just shrugged and said he didn't know, but he was glad to be there. When I asked about his name, Cujo winked and said it was a nickname. He said his real name was long and hard to pronounce. He also said that if we ever needed anything, we should let him know. He's made good on his offer. He's always giving me and Derek two-for-one coupons for plays and concerts happening in The Exchange, and he has an extra key and the security code for Auntie Sylvia's apartment in case we forget—which in the beginning we did.

Having a doorman was cool at first, but now—no offence to Cujo—I wish he wasn't there. He reminds me how everything is so different from the way it used to be, and that opens up a big hole inside me. Nothing can fill it up. Every minute of every day I feel this pain that begins—and ends—with Derek. I should only be sad about Mom and Dad dying. It's not fair that I'm too worried about Derek to hate him!

I understand the house fire was an accident, really I do. But part of me still wants to scream at him, tell him it's his fault! I want to say it to his face...but I can't. I'm afraid of my anger. It's like some crazy demon-beast inside me. If I let it out, it'll swallow everything, and I won't be able to take it back. I'm afraid it might drive Mom and Dad away. Even farther away than they are now. It's hard to explain...even to myself.

But that's why I can't say it out loud.

Turning into the back alley, I look for a quiet space where no one will see me. Pressing myself into an old wooden doorframe, not caring about splinters or flaking paint, I let myself cry. It has to come out sometimes. I know that. I sob until the burn of my rage settles into plain old sadness. I slide my back down the door until I'm sitting in the dirt, staring up at fragments of leftover rain cloud between the rooftops, blinking at the brightness. I close my eyes.

In Toronto when we were running together and I tried a vault or a cat-leap but didn't quite make it, Derek would laugh and tell me that the good thing about falling is that it gives you a chance to get back up again. He always pushed me to keep trying.

Now it's my turn to push him, I guess, except he's turned into a stubborn stupid rock. Not so easy to push. Maybe I don't have it in me.

Dusting myself off, I set off at a much slower pace than I usually do. I don't even know where I'm going. Just...somewhere. I walk and think about Derek. I walk and think about Mom and Dad. Doesn't Derek see that he's dishonoring them? Doesn't that matter to him?

Mom had been an infectious disease research scientist, and Dad was an ironworker. It's funny when you think about it. Mom spent most of her time hunched over a microscope looking at dangerous microbes—like the ones that caused SARS—and Dad walked metal grids on tall buildings high above all the sneezing disease-spewing heads. Each, in their own way, had a lot of guts. That's why they both went back into the house to save Derek. That's why they're both dead.

Maybe it isn't such a good thing to stick your neck out for people. Maybe if someone doesn't want saving, you should just let them be.

I blink. Putting one foot in front of the other I've landed, without planning to, at the corner where I usually cross to the river park and labyrinth. Seems that even if I don't know what I need, my body does. Running always makes me feel better. It settles my mind.

And so, I run.

chapter six

I jog down the hill to the labyrinth and find Angel on his bench. I wonder where he goes when he's not downtown.

"Hello," I call.

Like all the times before, he looks startled. Except this time he speaks. "How'd you make out?" he asks. It's an odd thing to say. Maybe he's not used to casual chitchat. At least he tried. We're making progress.

"Fine," I answer, smiling.

Turning back to the labyrinth, I sprint toward a wall. Standing tall on top, I fall into my usual routine of precision-jumping and cat-leaps. On the platform I ready myself for another round.

"It's way past six. Do you train *all* the time?"

Startled, I fall back on my heels. I have one arm outstretched and the other close to my body. It probably looks like I'm ready for a fight.

"Easy!" Rain says, as she steps out from behind the half-wall, laughing.

I lower my arms and shake my head. "I had another fight with my brother. Running makes me feel better."

Rain nods. "I get that. Whenever my mom and I fight, I like to get out and do something. Usually I go to the gymnastics club."

"Do you fight with your mom lots?"

Rain shrugs. "Usually only when I ask her to buy something for me. If she'd just quit smoking we'd have lots of money."

Rain looks at the river, eyes distant.

I don't know what to say. Money must be tight for Rain and her mom. "That sucks."

Rain sighs and looks at me, smiling brightly. "Want some company?"

I grin. "Sure...if you think you can keep up!"

Rain's eyes are suddenly shining. She spins on one foot and calls over her shoulder, "I followed you before. This time you can follow me!"

I follow Rain through the labyrinth and past Angel's now-empty bench. I like how easily Rain precision-jumps from one post to the next and then tic-tacs off of the brick wall. Two weeks of running and practicing moves together at her gym have helped Rain's technique.

It's been good for me too. I've worked on my upper-body strength by doing pull-ups and rope-climbing. Next time I try to climb a building I'll make it higher than the fourth floor.

As if reading my mind Rain veers away from the river park and toward The Exchange. But instead of heading toward the buildings we visited before, she crosses the main drag.

"Where are you going?" I call.

"Wait and see!"

We dodge shoppers and pigeons on the sidewalk. As swiftly as possible, we run along a street dotted with art and antique shops. Crossing the old market square, we run through the parking garage splashed with graffiti. The tagging inside is colorful and unexpected. Next to shiny purple lettering that says *Canada Rules* there's a painting of a sheep wearing sunglasses and a gas mask. Not far away there's more graffiti. A double *T* painted in black on a red circle makes me shiver—it's a gang-tag.

Aside from seeing the gang graffiti, the run is pleasant, if a bit boring. Rain isn't making any special effort to leap over anything, though it does look like she has a plan. Whatever. I'm happy to follow.

She turns left, then right, then left again until we finally stop in a back alley between two brick buildings. This time, instead of back stairs, each level has a balcony jutting out.

"More climbing?" I ask.

"Not just climbing," Rain says. "This time there will be a reward!"

"What do you mean?"

Rain cocks her head to one side. "What do you think is up there, Nikki?"

I look more closely this time. One of the buildings is old, with about a dozen weather-worn levels. The other is being renovated, probably to accommodate new condos like the one I now live in. Through balcony railings I can see that some units still have plastic-covered spaces where windows and doors will be. Some of the other apartments already look lived in, with nice planted pots and expensive-looking BBQs—the kind that can do everything but fly to Miami.

"Dirty socks and dust bunnies, same as any other apartment," I say.

"Wrong! Up there is everything we've ever wanted."

"I'm still not getting you, Rain."

"School starts in a month and a half."

"So?"

"Grade eleven is different from grade nine and ten. We're not little kids anymore."

"But what's that got to do with these apartments?"

Rain hesitates. "Money is power, Nik. Didn't anyone ever tell you that?"

I narrow my eyes. "What are you suggesting?"

Rain leans close. "We have the skills, and we make a good team. I'm saying we climb! Right now, before the people in these nice new condos get their security systems hooked up."

For a moment I can't speak. It feels like when I miss a landing and get the wind knocked out of me. "You want us to steal?"

Rain shrugs. "A few CDs. Small electronics. Stuff no one will miss for a while. Stuff we can sell."

I fall back a step. My mouth is open, but nothing is coming out.

"Look," Rain says. "I know a guy who will buy whatever we bring him, no questions asked. I get all my tech stuff from him, cheap." She glances over her shoulder and then back at me. "Close your mouth, Nik, unless you want to swallow a fly."

"What tech stuff? I didn't know this about you."

"I'm kind of a techno-geek."

Rain is grinning, as if she thinks it's funny and that I'll think so too.

I swallow. "I can't believe you're suggesting we steal." It hits me like a board over the back of the head. Has she only been pretending to be my friend? "How long have you been planning this?"

Rain looks uncomfortable. "For a while. What's the big deal?"

I shake my head. "I can't believe this."

"Think about it! It'll be just like in the movies. We'll be cat-leaping catburglars, making our escape over rooftops!"

"This isn't a movie, Rain. It's wrong."

"Just think about it. Think about how popular we'll be when school starts!"

"Because we're thieves?"

"No...that part we should keep secret. We'll be popular because we'll have coin for anything we want—clothes, Mp3 players, whatever."

"If anyone finds out about it, we'll end up with criminal records, Rain. Count me out."

"Because of your aunt? Because she's a judge?"

"No, because of me." Turning, I walk away. So much for friendship. Friends don't ask friends to steal. Should be on a T-shirt.

At the end of the alley, just before turning onto the street, I hear something. It breaks through the inner roar of my anger.

It's gone now...but I think it was a shout.

I turn and look back at Rain. She's standing where I left her, looking deeper into the alley.

Suddenly there's a scream, like the sound of an animal in great pain.

"Come on." Rain motions for me to join her. "It came from over there," she says, pointing farther down the alley.

"I don't see anything," I say, just loud enough for her to hear. I put my anger in a box and save it for later. All I can think about is the gang-tag I saw in the parking garage. Even though it's daylight, we're just far enough from the busy part of downtown for it to be dangerous.

"There's another alley back there," Rain whispers. "Come on."

"Are you crazy? We should get out of here!"

Rain opens her cat-eyes wider. "What if someone's hurt?"

Two sickening thuds followed by cries of anguish kill my doubt. Someone is getting beat up—we have to help! Staying close to the building on the left, we run deeper into the alley. Where the second alley connects, we peer carefully around the corner.

Rain grabs my arm, as if to stop me from revealing myself. Three men in baggy pants with red bandanas wrapped around their heads are beating someone crumpled on the ground between them. They're wearing jackets with the double *T* gang insignia. Gangbangers.

"Please...," the person on the ground cries. Before he can say anything else, one of the men kicks him in the belly. Whatever he was going to say comes out as a wheezy groan.

I know we should leave now and get help...but there's something about the attacker that is familiar. Have I seen him somewhere before? I wish I could see his face.

"Come on!" Rain whispers.

I nod, but before I can move, the kicker steps back, and I can see his victim.

Derek!

chapter seven

"That's my brother!" I groan, hardly able to get the sound out. I try to go to him, but again Rain holds me back.

"Stop! We'll go for help."

Except we don't move. We can't. We're frozen.

"Stay quiet," the kicker says, his voice harsh, "or you'll get more of that."

They start dragging Derek farther down the alley, away from us. The kicker turns, as if he can feel us watching him, and we duck.

I look again. I have to.

It's the guy with the ballcap who met Derek at the parking garage two weeks ago! I don't recognize the other two guys. One is stocky, with dark slicked back hair and a big nose. The other guy has stringy red hair and a purple scar stretching from his mouth to his ear.

Rain looks like she's seen a thousand horrors. I feel the same way. We peek back around the corner and wait until they disappear around the corner at the end of the alley. We follow, keeping our eyes and ears peeled for any sign they might turn around and come back. At the end of the alley, we peer cautiously into the street.

Rain points. "There!"

Just in time, I see them go up a set of stairs and into a building half a block away, on the other side of the street.

There are old, run-down, multi-leveled buildings on both sides of the street. The structures are so close together that they look like footballers shoulder-to-shoulder in a huddle. Some of them are even joined, and the only way you can tell they are separate is by the color or number of stories. The one Derek and the gangbangers have disappeared into is second from the end in a set of four. It looks like it was a neighborhood pub in better times. The sign above the front door is faded but still legible—*The Blue Turtle*.

The dirt-covered windows—one on each side of a solid door—are too high up to look through at street level. We wait to make sure no one is coming out, and then we dash across the street. I precision-jump onto a rail beside the steps and peer inside the window on the left. It's gloomy inside, but I can still make out an old bar along the back wall and a broken chair knocked over in the middle of the floor.

"What do you see?" asks Rain.

"Nothing—they must be in another room."

Rain leaps on the rail to the right and looks through the window on that side. "It's empty," she says.

"They have to be here somewhere," I say. I try the door, but it's locked. My heart is pounding so hard I can hear it. "Come on." Without waiting to see if Rain will follow, I dash around the corner down the right side of the block to look for a back entrance. Rain is right with me as we find the alley and then the back door. It's locked. There's a fire escape beginning at the second floor.

"He could be anywhere in there," Rain says, still whispering. "We should go for help."

"In a minute," I say. Rain is right—we need help—but I can't leave Derek. "What can we do against them?" Rain asks. "They're gang-bangers. They probably have guns."

"Let's find out exactly where they are first," I say.

I motion for Rain to wait. After a short sprint, I tic-tac off a wall and cat-leap to the lowest stair platform. On landing, I hit my knee against a metal bar and cringe as it clangs dully in the silence. I listen for a moment, half expecting to hear a battalion of footsteps coming from the belly of this building. Nope. Somewhere a car alarm goes off, and a man starts yelling, as if he's trying to out-shout the alarm. A woman starts yelling overtop of him.

Good. Maybe they'll help cover any sound I make.

I ignore the pain in my knee and climb over the rail. There's a dirty glass window in the door, but I can't see anything inside. I try the door. Like the other two, it's locked.

Climbing the stairs to the next level, I peer through the window in the door. Movement! It disappears, and I give my head a shake. Did I really see it? I cup my hands to block out the sun and strain my eyes. There's a light in the hall, but it isn't bright. It's coming from somewhere else. I see a door open at the end of the hall, on the right. The light is coming from there.

Suddenly the light is gone. Someone must have shut the door.

That must be where they took Derek. It has to be! The building looks pretty much deserted otherwise.

I try the door—locked. I glance from side to side. Like so many of the buildings in The Exchange, the outside is decorated with squares, knobs and freaky-looking heads. I remember they're called plasters. Usually I think they're cool. Today I think they're handy.

On the fourth floor, just above my head, there are tall windows with railings made to look like doors with fake balconies. They only come out a few inches. They're handy too.

Launching myself from the edge of the rail, I precision-jump to a plaster, spring off it and reach up for a window rail. Got it! My shoulders scream. With my legs swinging free beneath me, I think this might not be the brightest move I've ever made.

No stopping now.

Grunting, I swing my legs until I know the momentum will carry me; then I let go and grab the next window rail. My hands are sweaty and they pinch against the iron as they begin to slip. There are panic butterflies beating in my belly. I might fall.

Derek's cries ring in my ears.

Falling isn't an option.

I twist my grip, strengthening it. I make

myself imagine I'm swinging on monkey bars. That calms me. I'm as good as there.

Below me I see Rain's face—a pale circle, facing up.

I focus, swing and leap. Grasping the edge of the roof, I find a toe-hold against the brick and scrabble over the top. Whew! Without parkour, I wouldn't have made it. I brush grit from my knees and pull myself behind a large, arched, air duct. I'm on top of a building joined to the ones on either side—no gaps in between. To my left, The Blue Turtle building tops out at four levels. The building to my right is one level higher and has a metal-rung ladder attached to the side.

There are four windows and a door on The Blue Turtle building, as if this roof might have been its outdoor patio once upon a time. Maybe it was an art gallery, and people had fancy cocktail parties up here. A quick glance at the neighborhood makes me think maybe not. At least, not in a long time. I run, crouched over, peeking in each window. I see nothing until I get to the third window. I think this must be the room I saw the light coming from. Carefully, I peek inside.

He's here. They all are. I pull back, flattening myself against the building. My heart is pounding. I feel sick to my stomach.

Derek is tied to a chair in the middle of the room, his arms behind his back. He's slumped forward, as if in pain. The three men in bandanas are standing around him.

I look again.

Besides the chair Derek is in, there are a couple of couches, a table and a desk. The desk has a laptop computer and a printer on it. A large cardboard box is shoved against the wall.

The door opens. I duck away and then back again. No one is looking at the window. They're looking at a man at the door. I know him. It's the rock star guy I saw a few weeks back. Guess he found the address he was looking for.

Now it's my turn to be confused.

chapter eight

He isn't wearing gang colors or insignia, but the others greet him as if he belongs. He's got on the same skinny black jeans and snakeskin boots I saw him in last time, but this time he's wearing a red T-shirt under an oilskin duster.

I can hear voices through the glass, but they're muffled. The rock star moves toward Derek, hands on his hips. I want to cry out as he backhands Derek, hard. Derek's head snaps to the side.

"Who the hell are you?" Derek shouts. "What do you want?"

His voice is loud enough that I can hear him, even through the glass.

One of gangbangers steps forward and cuffs Derek. "His name's Spinner, punk! You better give him respect."

I can hear that too.

The man called Spinner takes out a cell phone, punches in some numbers and puts it to Derek's lips.

"Help me!" Derek cries. "Please help, I'm..."

Spinner smiles, as if he's gotten exactly what he wants; then he raises the phone to his mouth. He moves toward the corner of the room, where I can't see him. What's he doing? Who's he talking to?

The sound of the roof door opening sends me scrambling back on my haunches. The door is old and it sticks. It's like a gift! Just in time, I reach the duct and crouch behind it. Grasping the roof edge, I almost scream. Instead of crumbling brick I feel flesh. It's Rain! She's climbed up and is looking at me with wide cat eyes. I help her over the edge and put my finger to my lips. I point, and she nods her understanding.

Spinner is speaking into his phone. "Some people think the number three is lucky. Do you?" His voice is soft and silky, but cold. I shiver.

"The case comes before you at three o'clock this afternoon. It's just coming up on noon. That gives you three hours to consider the defense lawyer's motion and then dismiss all charges. If you don't, three is the number of hours your nephew has left to live." He flips the phone shut.

Every ounce of blood is leaving my body. I'm cold. Frozen. He's talking to Auntie Sylvia. He wants her to dismiss charges. But why? For who? Then I remember the difficult case Auntie Sylvia has been working on. The one about the bad cop.

Warm fingers touch mine, bringing me back. Rain. Her eyes are huge. She looks like she's trying not to cry.

I peek around the duct. Spinner is at the front edge of the roof, looking down at the street. The guy who kicked Derek in the alley joins him at the front of the roof. He stands behind Spinner, as if waiting to be noticed.

"We're on, Billy," Spinner says, turning to face him.

Billy smiles. It's not a friendly smile. Maybe he means it to be, but to me he looks one of those puffed-up spiny lizards getting ready to eat something. "This is going to be huge."

"Yes, it is, Billy. Not only will the execution of our little operation elevate me to a status I so rightfully—"

"And me too, right, Spinner?"

Annoyance flashes across Spinner's face. "Didn't your mother teach you any manners, Billy?"

Billy looks uncomfortable.

Spinner sighs loudly. "Yes, Billy, you'll get what's coming to you—you and your band of merry thugs. But as I was saying before I was so rudely interrupted, not only will our operation put us on top, but some might say we are doing our civic duty."

"How do you mean?"

"Why, Billy, we are revitalizing the downtown core! It's what everyone whines about."

"I don't think our grow-ops are quite what they had in mind."

"Be that as it may, what we are doing is bringing life to these decrepit old buildings. Plant life. Besides, cash flow is always good for a neighborhood."

"As long as the judge cooperates."

"She had better, Billy. In order to stay healthy, we need our guy back on the outside."

"But won't they be watching him?"

It was Spinner's turn to smile. His smile is much more menacing than Billy's. "I'm referring to *our* health, Billy, not his."

Billy pauses, as if trying to work that out. I'm thinking it's pretty clear. Auntie Sylvia has to set the bad cop free, so that Spinner can...get rid of him. I shiver.

"Okay, Spinner," Billy finally says. "I gotcha. As long as our guy is in custody, there's a chance he'll tell what he knows. We can't have that happen."

"That's good, Billy. Guess your mother didn't raise an idiot after all. Ill-mannered, yes, but not an idiot." Spinner turns his back on him and looks back to the street. "Now go. You know what to do."

Billy nods and goes back inside.

Spinner just stands, like a king looking out over his kingdom. The sight of him, all smug, like he owns the city, makes me want to run up and push him over the edge.

He turns and follows Billy inside, but as the door scrapes against the doorframe it doesn't quite shut. I make sure Rain sees it. She nods and puts a finger to her lips. I return to the window.

Spinner isn't there, but Billy is facing the others. "Spinner is a freaking genius," he says. He looks at Derek, who is now slumped over in his chair, with a trickle of blood running down his face. He laughs and turns back to the others. "Only he would know how to turn this into an opportunity. I gotta go plant our insurance. If something goes wrong, kill the kid."

The scarred-up guy with stringy red

hair steps forward. "Spinner told the judge three."

"Are you gonna argue with me, Cutter?"

Cutter looks like he's thinking about it for a moment, and then he shakes his head. "No, but I don't want to be crossing Spinner, man. I don't think that's wise."

"Relax. Spinner told me it was okay. Someone comes, this dude's dead. Otherwise, he's got till three."

I gulp.

After Billy leaves, the others relax. They look like they'll be there for a while. I back away and scuttle over to Rain.

"Holy crap," Rain whispers.

I nod, and my eyes suddenly fill with tears. "Derek is in big trouble."

"Yeah. So who's this guy they were talking about?"

Quickly, I explain about the special court and the case Auntie Sylvia's been working on.

Rain grabs hold of my arm. "Come on. Now that we know where Derek is, we can get help!"

"Not yet," I say. My voice comes out weak, even for a whisper. "He told the guys that if anyone comes, or if something goes wrong, they're to kill Derek. As long as no one get's in their way, Derek is okay until three."

Rain leans against the duct, shaking her head. "Craptastic."

I take a deep breath. "Billy said he's going to plant some sort of insurance."

"What does that mean?"

"I don't know, but I think I should follow him. You stay here and watch, okay? Maybe when I get back we'll have a better idea about what we should do."

"Be careful."

I hesitate. It makes me feel better to know someone's keeping watch, but how much can I trust Rain? Back in the alley she pretty much destroyed any faith I had in her.

I give my head a shake. It's not like I have a choice. Besides, this isn't about stealing CDs. It's about Derek's life. Even Rain must know the difference.

"We'll get him out of this," Rain says. I wish I felt as sure as Rain sounds.

I nod and swing myself over the edge. Unlike the building next door, this building has windows with thick wooden frames. Rain must have had an easy time climbing up to join me. I cat-leap all the way to the ground.

I retrace my steps back to the street just in time to catch sight of Billy disappearing around the corner. At a safe distance, I follow. When he reaches a street with normal daytime traffic and shoppers, I follow more closely. I shove my hands in my hoodie pockets and pretend to be looking in shop windows or at my feet.

One more turn and a suspicion tickles me. Actually, it's more like a pinch. One turn after that and I'm sure. Billy is going to our condo building!

But why? Even if he has Derek's key, Cujo won't let him pass. And what about the alarm in the apartment?

I stay at the corner, watching from around the red brick edge. There's Cujo, looking straight ahead. His hands are clasped behind his back, just like always. As Billy approaches him, Cujo turns away. What the...? Cujo must have seen him coming—why did he turn his back? As if it is the most natural thing in the world, Billy walks past Cujo. Weird. Why wouldn't he open the door for him? After all, that's what a doorman does. It's like he's pretending not to see him...except I'm sure he did.

I see Cujo turn and watch the door shut behind Billy. This can only mean one thing.

Cujo is in on it.

chapter nine

I press myself into the brick.

Cujo should have asked Billy who he was there to see. It was just that kind of building—exclusive. But with his back turned, he could pretend he didn't see Billy—no questions asked. Later he would be able to plead innocence.

Except I saw him turn and watch the door close after Billy. He's not so innocent. He probably even gave him the key. Our spare key.

I'm too shocked to be angry, but I know I will be soon. What a jerk! How can he betray us like this? What did we ever do to him?

Peering back around the corner, I see he's still there staring straight ahead, hands behind his back. As if nothing has happened.

But something has happened. Spinner threatened Auntie Sylvia. She has to corrupt herself or Derek will die. It's an awful threat, but I know she'll do what Spinner demands. What choice does she have?

Why is Billy going up to our apartment? I have to find out. It's a good thing I have my own way of getting past Cujo.

I sprint away from our building, cross the street and go around the block. As I turn the last corner I smash into a guy on a bike. We're a tangle of metal, tires and limbs, but I'm not hurt. He's okay too, except for being a bit surprised, maybe. He looks at me with eyes the color of a bright new penny. They remind me of wolf eyes. Annoyed wolf eyes. "Sorry, sorry!" I yelp, untangling myself. "Sorry," I say one more time as I continue my dash into the alley next to my building.

It's easier to build momentum coming from the other direction, but I can still get into our condo this way. Climbing The Zloty has become something I can almost do in my sleep.

Stretching myself from a window frame to a balcony, I precision-jump to the next balcony and climb up one more. Finally I pull myself up to Auntie Sylvia's place and press myself against the building. Is Billy inside? I sneak a quick look. I don't see him. Not yet.

My aunt isn't home, but even if the balcony door isn't locked I don't dare open it. Only the front door has a sixty-second delay that allows the person coming in to deactivate the alarm. There's no delay on the balcony door. If the alarm is set, and I open the door, the alarm will go off and the police will come. That can't happen. Nothing can get in Billy's way or interfere with Spinner's plans. Not yet. That would be bad news for Derek.

Even if the alarm hasn't been set, a warning beep will sound when I open the door. If Billy *is* already inside, or even in the hall outside the apartment, he'll hear it. Most of the suite is open concept, with only the bathroom and three bedrooms closed off. The kitchen, which is open to the living room, is right beside the balcony. There's no kitchen island or anything for me to duck behind.

I look again. I don't see anything at first, but then Billy comes out of Auntie Sylvia's room. If he's already inside that means Derek either forgot to set the alarm or Billy disarmed it. Cujo probably gave him the code.

He takes a long look at the kitchen and living room, pulls out a screwdriver and removes an air vent casing from the wall. He sets it carefully to the side. From his inside jacket pocket he takes out something green and shaped like a brick, and a tall stack of bills. The brick looks weird, like it's made up of compacted grass. It hits me—it's marijuana! Must be from the grow-ops Spinner was talking about.

Billy strokes the brick for a moment and shakes his head before placing it and the money in the air vent. He replaces the cover and tightens the screws.

This is their insurance? What are they

thinking...that they can make Auntie Sylvia look like she's involved in the grow-ops? I gulp as I think about what might happen next. If Auntie Sylvia does what Spinner wants, she *will* be involved. No going back.

Spinning on his heel, Billy moves to the door, punches a number code into the alarm unit and leaves.

He knows our alarm code. I take a moment to imagine horrible things happening to Cujo. Maybe he'll die a slow painful death while crows peck out his eyeballs and maggots burst from his intestines. It's what he deserves.

Now what? Do I call the cops, or do I go back to Rain and Derek? Except I can't call the cops—I don't know who's honest and who's corrupt. My indecision screams at me. I feel like I'm caught up in a crazy bad dream, the kind where you try and wake up but can't. Instead you fall deeper and deeper into it.

What would Derek do?

Derek would say that sometimes you can think too much.

The alarm is still counting down. I wait only as long as I think it will take for Billy to get on the elevator or into the stairwell, and then I fling open the balcony door. The door alarm beeps twice more before I reach it and disarm it. I chance a look down the hall. Billy is gone.

Racing to the phone, I dial Auntie Sylvia's cell phone. If she's unable to answer, the call will be forwarded to her office receptionist. While I wait for Auntie Sylvia to pick up, I open the kitchen drawer where I usually toss my own cell phone when I'm out running. I retrieve it and tuck it in my hoodie pocket.

Auntie Sylvia's line is busy. I press Disconnect and stab the Redial button.

I'm about to hang up on a second busy signal and redial, when I realize it doesn't sound quite right. It's like it's in double-time. Is there something wrong with the line? Just as I think it, the line goes dead. I disconnect and hit Redial one more time. Same thing.

What is up with the phone lines? There's no time to puzzle it out. I've got to move! I leave the apartment the way I entered it— over the balcony. I don't want to even *look* at Cujo. Besides, if he sees me he'll guess I've been to the apartment, and that will be bad for Derek.

I hope, I hope, I hope that Derek is still okay. But what if they catch Rain watching them? My stomach goes into lock-down, and I feel a ball of panic settle in the middle of it. As I round a corner, I miss a step and almost fall.

Billy!

He's standing on a corner outside a jewelry store, not ten feet away. His back is to me, and he's searching the street, as if looking for someone.

I hunch into the deep entrance of a shop with a hanging sign saying *Aslan and Frodo's Used Books*. To avoid attention, I pretend to read the posters in the window. I don't dare try and leave, but I keep my hand on the door, ready to dash inside should Billy turn my way.

With a jangle the door opens, smashing into me. Man! I look up and see the same guy I crashed into earlier—those wolf eyes are hard to miss. He helps me up, apologizing. I

Anita Daher

whisper, "It's okay," and try to press deeper into the doorway.

"Okay then," the guy says, strapping a bicycle helmet over springy black curls. As he rides away I hear him mutter, "Karma."

I glance at Billy before turning back to the posters. He's still looking up and down the street. Good.

A moment later a car slows, and Billy hops in. I recognize the car—it's the green Corvette. I can't see the driver.

As soon as the Corvette is out of sight, I take off as if I'm running the final leg of a relay race. In the back alley, I toss a stone to the roof, hoping to see Rain pop her head over the edge.

Nothing.

I toss another stone.

Maybe Rain is watching Derek and can't see—or hear—the stones.

Actually, at this moment it would be hard to hear anything, as a city garbage truck groans its way into the alley. The Blue Turtle building looks empty, but other buildings still house offices and shops. I can't help wondering if they are normal businesses or if some of Spinner's grow-ops are in there.

I wait until the garbage crew has moved off before I climb the building and heave myself onto the roof.

Rain isn't there.

A quick check of the window confirms my fears. Derek and the gangbangers are gone!

Racing to the front of the roof, I look as far as I can in both directions. A hand grips my shoulder, and I scream.

chapter ten

Another hand immediately clamps over my
mouth. I twist away, ready to fight, until I see
cat eyes, filled with fear.

"For god's sake, be quiet!" Rain hisses.

My eyes are moist. "I thought they'd
caught you!" My knees buckle. "I didn't know
what to do."

"They moved Derek," Rain says in a rush.
"I tried to keep up, but I couldn't."

I feel the color draining from my face, and
I'm cold and dizzy. I want to curl up in a ball

and cry. But that won't help my brother. I gulp. "We need to call my aunt."

"Forget your aunt, just call the police!"

"Not the police. We can't."

"Why not?" Rain asks. Then she slaps her forehead. "Oh...right. The big police corruption case."

"What if we call the cops and it's one of the bad ones? It's my aunt or no one!" I pull out my cell phone. "Auntie Sylvia's number wasn't working before, but maybe it's okay now."

"While you're calling let's check out this place."

The back door is still open a crack. I punch numbers on the cell phone as I follow Rain inside and watch as she pulls open the cardboard box.

One ring.

"Holy crap!" Rain cries, pulling out a small rectangle of black plastic with metal trim. It's small enough to fit in the palm of her hand. She holds it so I can see it. The nameplate says *Stickler.*

Two rings.

"What is it?"

"A personal GPS. You know—Global Positioning System."

Three rings.

"How do you know?"

"I told you, I'm a techno-geek. Remember that guy I told you about? The guy I buy stuff from?"

Four rings.

"Anyway, he's got tons of cool stuff. I haven't seen a GPS exactly like this," she says, dropping the Stickler back in the box, "but I'll bet you a million dollars that's what it is. That laptop over there probably has a program that maps the signals."

Five rings. Enough! I'm about to hang up when someone picks up.

"Sylvia Gurniak's office," a man's voice says. It's a pleasant voice but unexpected. Auntie Sylvia must have forwarded her calls to her office receptionist, but every other time I've called the receptionist has been a woman.

"Sylvia Gurniak, please."

"I'm sorry, but she's not available," the voice says. "Would you like to leave a message?"

"No...yes! It's an emergency. Can you tell

her it's Nikki and that I need to talk to her right now?"

Rain has stopped looking through the box and is watching me.

"I'm sorry, but she's unavailable," the voice repeats. Whoever it is, his tone is soothing. It's also familiar.

"It's important! Can you tell her it's about Derek? He's been kidnapped!"

"Who is this?" the voice says, suddenly harsh.

I snap the phone shut and drop it like it's a burning coal.

"What's wrong?" Rain asks.

"It was Spinner," I say, my mind whirling. "It doesn't make sense. Why is he at the court-house answering Auntie Sylvia's phone?"

Rain frowns. "Maybe he's not really there."

"What do you mean?"

"There's more than Sticklers in that box. Some of that stuff is pretty high-tech. They're probably intercepting your aunt's phone calls."

"We have to go to her."

"Wait! Let's check the laptop first."

"We don't have time!"

"But knowing why Spinner has all these Sticklers might help us."

"Oh..." I breathe, finally understanding. "You think he's tracking Billy and the other guys?"

"It's worth a shot. If he is, it might lead us to Derek."

It's so confusing...my head feels like it's being swarmed by gnats. But there's no time to think it through. "Okay...okay, maybe you're right. Let's boot it up. Now!"

I put my cell phone back in my pocket and watch as Rain powers up the laptop.

"Hurry!"

"I am."

Finally the desktop appears. "How do we find the program?"

"I'm guessing this icon with the evil-looking spy eyes might be it. Cross your fingers!" She double clicks.

S T I C K L E R flashes across the screen.

"Yeah!" I cry. But my triumph is crushed

a second later as a box with the instructions *Enter Password* appears.

"Crap!" Rain cries, pounding her fist on the desk.

I look at her. "Can you figure it out?"

"I'm good, but not that good."

The laptop makes a small whirling sound.

"Wait," I say. My stomach is so tight you could bounce a quarter off it. "It's doing something."

We watch as five stars appear where the password should be.

Rain is grinning. "Idiots."

Using the touch pad, Rain drags the cursor from one heading to the next. One reads *Tracks*. She double-clicks on it. A column appears. She reads it aloud. "Badger, Billy, Cutter, Elvis, Cujo."

"We know who Billy and Cutter are," I say, frowning. "And Cujo is the doorman."

"What doorman?"

"He's works at our building. I think he's in on it." Quickly, I tell her what I saw. "Looks like Spinner doesn't trust his crew very much, if he's tracking them."

Rain shrugs. "Can't trust anyone if you're building a grow-op empire. It's good news for us, anyway. If the guys who have Derek are being tracked, we should be able to find out where they went."

She clicks on Cutter's name. A map appears showing a thick red line crisscrossing back and forth. Rain moves the cursor to the side of the page and selects a time range showing the past hour. "That's better."

"Holy, that's clear!" I cry. It looks as if someone took a picture from a low-flying airplane or maybe a helicopter.

"It's a satellite picture," Rain explains. "If the GPS unit is turned on, it sends out a base signal to a satellite. The satellite sends it back to the receiving unit—the laptop."

"Check the other tracks—just to make sure there's two the same. If they split up, it'll take longer to find Derek." I wait until she clicks through each one.

"The tracks for Badger and Cutter match," Rain announces.

"As long as they don't move again, it looks like they're still in The Exchange."

"Looks like Cujo is on the move now too," she says, clicking on his name.

"Cujo can wait. Print us the map for Badger and Cutter, and let's go!"

While the printer hums and spits, Rain moves back to the cardboard box. "Should we take the box?"

"How can you think of stealing now, Rain? My brother's life is at stake!"

Rain's face darkens. "I know that," she says, "but I wasn't thinking about me. This stuff is worth a lot of money. It could be a bargaining chip."

I know I should feel terrible for suspecting Rain, but I'm too worried about Derek. "I'm sorry," I say. "Maybe you're right, but let's be quick!"

As the printer works on the map, I glance around the room one more time. What else should we take? The laptop, for sure! I open the desk drawer. Inside I see a box of bullets. It's empty.

I should be terrified, but I'm not. Not as much as I was when Derek was first snatched, anyway. At first I believed Billy—that Spinner is some kind of freaking criminal genius. But now I'm thinking even smart criminals make mistakes. Like using an automatic password on the Stickler program. This makes me feel better—stronger.

I'm not very happy about the bullet box, though. It's a reminder of how dangerous these guys really are. We need to be careful.

Rain picks up the cardboard box and glances at the printer. "The map is ready."

I fold the map and tuck it in my pocket next to my cell phone; then I grab the laptop and follow Rain to the front door. With all this stuff it'll be easier to take the stairs.

"Wait," I say. "Better check the hall first."

Rain sets the box down and opens the door. I'm right on her heels. A sudden high-pitched sound almost makes me drop the laptop. It sounds like air escaping out of a pinprick hole in a balloon. I look up. Above the door there's a small camera pointed directly at us. It has a tiny red light on it. The light is blinking.

chapter eleven

"Spinner has the place wired!" I shout, jumping out of the camera view.

"Yeah, but probably not with any legit alarm companies. Let's go!" Rain dashes back to the box and picks it up.

"Wait—out the back. They used the front door before. If they're coming after us, we don't want to run into them!"

Rain nods and follows me out.

This time, instead of dropping into the back alley, I point to the ladder on the other building. "Up there!"

It's awkward climbing up the ladder with the laptop. I have Rain pass me up the laptop and the box once I'm on the next roof. Just as Rain climbs over the top, we hear squealing tires. On our hands and knees, we crawl to the edge of the roof and look down at the street in front of The Blue Turtle. The green Corvette screeches to a stop and two guys jump out. One is the guy with the stocky build and slicked-back hair we saw earlier. The other has thick sideburns crawling down the sides of his face, like mutant black caterpillars.

"We can follow them to Derek!"

"We don't need them," Rain says. "We've got the map, remember? Let's get out of here!"

Rain is right. We're fully exposed if one of those guys decides to come up the ladder and take a look. We dash to the far side. It's a drop of about ten feet to the roof of the next building, which is also joined to this one. No problem. "Wait a second," I say. Setting the laptop at my feet, I leap, landing with my knees bent and rolling out. No problem.

"Toss me the laptop first," I call, keeping my voice as low as I can.

"Don't drop it!" Rain warns.

Her aim is good, and I don't.

"What about the box?" Rain asks. "I'm afraid it might fall apart if I throw it."

From close by, I can hear shouting. Spinner's thugs must have discovered the missing stuff and come out the back door after us! Rain hears it too, lowers the box down to me as far as she can and lets go. Without waiting to see if I catch it—which I do—she jumps and rolls out beside me.

This roof has an arched section toward the front of the building facing the street but is otherwise flat. No place to hide here either. I see there's a gap of about three feet between this building and the next. I've never roof-hopped before and would rather not start now, if there's any other way. Looking between the buildings, I spot a Dumpster at the end by the alley. I run to the back of the roof and see a fire escape leading part of the way down. "Here!" I say.

We climb down the staircase as far as we can and then use the Dumpster as a step.

"Now what?" Rain says, breathless. She's looking up and down the alley. So am I. No sign that we have been spotted—yet.

"We need to stash this stuff and get out of here," I say. "Here—in this Dumpster!"

"You're kidding me, right?"

"The garbage crew has already come through—remember? It'll be perfect!"

I lift the lid and something inside my stomach tries to crawl out my throat. I have to look away, as I wave the lid up and down, trying to air it out. Rain pinches her nose. "Smells like something died in there," she says.

"Which makes it perfect," I gasp. While Rain holds the lid open, I take a big gulp of good air and then lean into the Dumpster, carefully lowering the cardboard box, then the laptop. I pull some soggy newspapers over everything. Together, Rain and I lower the lid, making sure it doesn't clang.

We needn't have worried. The sound of squealing tires and a flash of green at the end of the narrow space between the buildings tells us Spinner's thugs have given up the search—on foot at least. They're either searching on wheels or going back to wherever they came from.

Spinner isn't going to be happy when he finds out his stuff is missing.

I hope we haven't made things worse for Derek.

A quick look at my watch twists my stomach in a knot. It's 1:10! I force myself to breathe deeply: in—one, two; out—one, two. I tell myself it's okay. We still have close to two hours. I turn to Rain. "We've got to tell my aunt."

Side by side, we run toward the special court, sticking to alleys and watching for another flash of green. As we near the old market square a worry begins tapping in my brain like a tiny silver hammer. A few seconds later it has the weight of a wrecking ball.

"Wait!" I cry, grabbing hold of Rain's arm.

"What is it?"

"What if they're watching the courthouse?

It would make sense, right? They'll want to know if Auntie Sylvia leaves or sends the police after them."

"But you said the police are corrupt."

"Not all of them. They couldn't be!"

"Would your aunt take that chance?"

"I don't know. The thing is, thanks to that camera feed, they probably already know our faces; they'll be watching for us. We need to think this through."

"Do we have time to think?"

"No. Let's go find Derek. Once we see what we're up against, we can figure out how to get a message through to my aunt. There has to be a way."

I pull out the map, and we check the Stickler path again. "Got it?" I ask Rain. She nods. The image is clear. Derek is being held in an old warehouse close to the river.

The old market square is crowded as we run through it. I vault over a bench, ignoring an angry shout. Rain is right behind me. We don't slow—we can't. Because I train every day, sometimes twice a day, I'm not even winded as we cross the main drag. Rain is in pretty good shape too. We race past the concert hall into the theater district. Rain follows easily as I tic-tac off a wall, over a fence and land, knees bent, in a construction zone. A few feet away, the construction gives way to a vacant lot strewn with building supplies. Across the lot there is an old green warehouse. Unlike other buildings in the area, it's a single story with a flat roof. Derek is inside. He has to be!

The construction site is empty and it doesn't have that fresh-cut lumber smell. We sidle along Dumpsters and crates until we finally reach the warehouse. Keeping a wary eye toward the front of the building, I dart forward along the left side of it to the closest window. I look inside.

Empty.

A hand on my shoulder makes me jump.

I take a deep breath. It's only Rain.

"It's too dangerous here," she whispers. "Someone might see. Let's check the back."

I nod and duck around to the less exposed back of the building, where there are two windows. I look in one, while Rain checks the other. Through my window I see a room with two sagging couches and a refrigerator. In a hall just beyond the door I see a man. I duck out of sight, even though he wasn't looking at the window. I peek again. He's gone.

"Just a storage room here," Rain says. "Nothing but boxes and shelves."

There's nothing left for us to see and we can go no farther.

"Should we circle around to the front?" Rain asks.

"Either that," I look to the roof, "or we try up there."

Not too far away, I hear a train. The old Union Train Station is at The Forks, and the tracks run right through The Exchange. The noise, combined with the usual street traffic, will give us a bit of cover. But not for long.

"Come on!" I sprint for the fence, tic-tac off it and scramble onto the warehouse roof. Right behind me I hear Rain tic-tac off the fence. I freeze as she screeches and falls in a heap beside me.

chapter twelve

My first thought is that we've been spotted, and Rain has been shot. But then I see Rain groaning and holding her ankle. She must have landed wrong.

"I'm sorry, Nikki!" she gasps. "Do you think someone heard?"

I listen hard as I pad softly to the edge of the building. As the train rumbles away, I don't hear any shouting. Nothing close by, anyway.

"I don't think so," I say as I rush back to her. "Are you okay?"

"I don't know. I landed pretty hard."

"Is it sprained?"

"It's twisted for sure," she says, gingerly testing her weight on it. "I'll have to see if it swells."

I look around. The roof is flat. Close to the middle there is an old skylight. It's set in a box, framed with wood and angled downward on the top. The window-glass is actually made of cloudy fiberglass. I tiptoe toward it. Rain follows, limping.

The skylight has hinges on one long side and a broken lock on the other. I grasp the edges and lift.

The first thing I notice is the humidity. It wafts out, carrying the scent of green growing things.

The next thing I notice is Spinner! Or at least the top of his head.

I ease the cover back down, heart pounding. He hasn't seen me. As long as he doesn't look up, we're okay. I lift the lid again—just enough so that we can see over the edge.

Spinner is standing in a room filled with leafy green plants in pots. And lights. Lots and lots of lights. Just above the low-hanging lights I can see canisters the size of small hot-water tanks. They're making a low humming sound.

Rain and I exchange looks. In my mind I give a low whistle—I don't dare make a sound out loud. This must be one of his grow-ops— his downtown core revitalization project.

Suddenly the door swings open, and the two guys who were chasing us burst in. Spinner turns to face them. He's got one hand on his hip, and he's tapping his foot.

"You know I've been waiting. Would it have killed you to call?"

"We were looking for those kids," the stocky guy says, "but we couldn't find them." His head is bowed slightly, his hands in his pants pockets.

"Idiots!" Spinner explodes, waving his arms in front of him. "You were there within seconds. How could they possibly get away?"

"That's what we thought too!" the fellow with the sideburns says. "Especially seeing as they were carrying all our..."

The first man kicks him, shutting him up.

Spinner lowers his arms to his sides and looks back and forth between them.

"Is there something you would like to tell me, Elvis?" Spinner asks the second man, his voice soft. "How about you, Badger?" he says, turning to the stocky guy.

Elvis looks at Badger. "We gotta tell him."

"They got some of our stuff," Badger admits.

"What stuff?"

"They grabbed the box and the laptop," Elvis says.

"The laptop? You morons!" Spinner roars. "I should have known about this immediately."

"So what about the laptop?" Elvis squeaks. "You've got a mobile unit for the Sticklers."

"Forget the Sticklers and everything else in the box. The information on that laptop will bury us."

"How?" Badger asks.

Spinner sighs noisily. "The files on that laptop. It's all there. My grow-op records and the Stickler maps to show where the grow-ops are."

Elvis looks confused. "Records? Why would you put...?"

"You dare question me?" Spinner's neck suddenly turns flaming red, like he's going to have the worst sunburn of his life.

"Uh, no, it's just..."

"Smart businessmen keep good records. Understand?"

"Yes." Elvis looks like he just swallowed something bad.

"It's okay, Spinner," Badger says. His voice is soothing. "They're just kids..."

"Precisely. And if, through their ignorance, that information falls into the wrong hands, I'm ruined."

Just kids...Spinner doesn't realize who we are! I think back. Spinner knew it was me on the phone, but I could have been calling from anywhere. From what he's saying, it sounds like Spinner thinks what happened at their office was a random break-in.

Funny. Spinner's wrong person is my right one. The problem is neither one of us likes our odds.

"Enough!" he snaps. "Tell Cutter to move the boy to the pump station."

I glance at Rain, who looks as worried as I feel. We run past the pump station all the time. It's not far from here. What worries me is that Spinner is changing his plan. I glance at my watch. It's 1:40. At least we know that Derek is still alive. For now, anyway.

"Okay, Spinner," Elvis says, his voice meek.

"You two get back and clean out that damn office! I want it so clean it squeaks. There should be no sign we were ever there. You got me, Elvis?"

"Yeah, Spinner." Elvis looks like he wants to puke.

"And find those kids!"

As Spinner follows them out, he slams the door shut behind him.

"I'm calling nine-one-one," I say, as I lower the window of the skylight and pull out my cell phone.

"You can't!" Rain cries. "We don't know who's involved, remember?"

"I don't care! We have to do something.

Spinner sounded crazy mad. Maybe he won't wait until three."

Rain swallows and nods.

"Besides, nine-one-one calls are recorded," I say. "They wouldn't dare mess with those."

My heart is pounding hard as I punch in the numbers. Fear is making my hands shake, and I'm hitting the wrong ones. I clear the number and try again. I hear a ring, but then the sound sort of stutters and stops.

What the...?

"No!" I cry, smashing the cell phone against the frame of the skylight.

"What's wrong?"

"Battery died. I always forget to charge it! I'll have to go to a store or something."

"Do we have time?"

"No...but what else can we do?"

"Think about it," Rain says. "We have something Spinner wants. Sounds like he wants it real bad."

Rain's is the voice of reason cutting through my confusion.

"You're right. Plus, he obviously doesn't know who we are. That's got to work in our favor." I sit and lean against the skylight. "Okay, let's figure this out. What have we got?"

"You mean besides the laptop and the Sticklers?"

I smile. "No, that's all we need. It's time to blow a hole in Spinner's empire."

chapter thirteen

"Be careful, Nik," Rain says.

"You be *more* careful," I say as I hug her close. "And take care of your ankle!"

I leap from the roof and roll out, checking to make sure the coast is clear. Sprinting across the lot, I feel my spirits lift. It feels good to run. It feels even better to have a plan. Actually, we have two plans. Plan A is better than Plan B, but between the two, we'll get this done. We have to.

I'm scared. Derek used to say it's important

to know your fear but not let it stop you. It won't. We're going to get him out. Not only that, but we're going to beat Spinner and his crew of idiots. Spinner will be sorry he ever messed with us.

At the concert hall, people gawk as I jump from the concrete partition to the open space below and vault over round tables—the empty ones. I hop the wall on the other side. On the corner I halt, toes at the curb, waiting for the traffic light. I hate waiting! But I can't risk getting hit by a car...or gaining unwanted attention.

I chew on my bottom lip and wonder. Is someone really watching the courthouse? Who? Where is he? Even if Spinner doesn't recognize me, Cujo will. If Cujo is the one watching, I'm in trouble.

Across the street I turn south, toward the special court. Two blocks from it, I sit on a bench and bend as if adjusting my sneaker. I look sideways, scanning the street. There's plenty of traffic going north and south. A lane is closed because of road construction, making it even more congested than usual. I see police guards in front of the building.

Are they good cops or bad ones?

I glance up and down the street, trying to think of the best way to get past the guards and any watchers. Luck. That's what I need. Just a little.

Out of the corner of my eye, a mass of rumpled gray is shuffling toward me.

Luck—or maybe a guardian angel!

Angel stops and sits next to me on the bench.

"Hello," I say.

"Hello," he replies, clearly but a little shyly. Unlike the first time we spoke, he's found the right response. Maybe he's been practicing.

I give him a small worried smile. After a moment, he smiles back. If things weren't so desperate, I might have felt pleased.

"Can you help me with something?" I ask. "It won't be hard, but it's important."

"Yes," he says, drawing the word out, as if thinking about it. "I can help you."

I pull the folded map from my hoodie pocket. "Can you take a note to my aunt?

She's a judge in that special courthouse. If you tell them it's an emergency, they should let you through."

"Are you in trouble, then?"

"No, but someone's life depends on this."

He looks at me sharply and then nods twice. Like he really means it. "I can help you."

"Um...I don't suppose you have a pen?"

He reaches into his jacket pocket and pulls out a pencil.

"Perfect! Thanks."

We found Derek, I write on the edge of the map. *He was at a grow-op here*. I circle the warehouse and draw an arrow to it. Then I draw another arrow to the pump station. *He's at the pump station now*, I write. *There are at least five guys involved, plus their leader. His name is Spinner.*

I look at my watch. It's 2:15. I fold the map, and hand it—and the pencil—to Angel. "It's for Judge Gurniak," I say. "I'm Nikki by the way."

"Hello, Nikki," Angel says. "I'm Ted."

"Hello, Ted," I say, flashing a quick smile. "I always call you 'Angel' in my head."

There's a spark in Ted's eyes, and he smiles back. "You can call me Angel, Nikki. I don't mind."

"Thank you. You're a lifesaver, you know."

He winks. "Actually, I'm a retired cop."

Huh! You just never know.

As he gets up to leave, I put my hand on his arm. "Be careful, Angel. Some of the good guys might not be so good."

He nods. "I know, Nikki. I've been following the news. Don't worry. I know what to say."

As Angel shuffles toward the special court, I search up and down the street, hoping no one has noticed me. If anyone has, I can't see who—or where. I wait, my elbow on my knee and my hand on my forehead, as if I have a headache. Out of the corner of my eye, I see Angel speak with one of the police guards. The guy nods and talks into a handheld radio. After a few seconds another cop emerges from the building. He says something to Angel. Angel turns and walks away.

Oh no!

Instead of returning to the bench, he shuffles to the first corner and turns in the direction of the old market square.

Leaving the bench, I mingle with other walkers and move away from the special courthouse. When I reach the corner, I turn toward the old market square and run. At the next block, I spin south again, looking for Angel. He's there. He's waiting for me.

"What did they say?" I ask, breathless, though not from running.

"Wouldn't let me in."

I set my jaw. It'll have to be Plan B, then. "Thanks anyway, Angel. I've got to run!"

"I'll keep trying," he says. "I know some people. Maybe I can still get this to her."

I feel like hugging him, but I don't want to scare him. Our friendship is still pretty new. Instead, I squeeze his hand. "Thanks, Angel. You take care, okay?"

"I always do."

I leave him and sprint across the park. My

eyes feel as wide as cereal bowls—I'm trying to look everywhere at once. Badger and Elvis might be somewhere close. I can't risk them seeing me.

When I reach the block where The Blue Turtle is, I tic-tac off the side of the two-story building on the end. After precisioning onto a cement ledge, I cat-leap and grab the broad edge of a window frame, climb and then scramble up over it to the roof. It feels safer up here than below.

I have five roofs to hop and climb to get back to the place where we left the laptop, and there are two three-foot gaps between two of the buildings. The rest of the buildings are all joined. It's probably a good thing I don't have time to worry about falling. I just do it and roll out. No problem. Finally I'm on the roof where I will climb down the fire escape to the Dumpster—just like before.

First...I've got to look. I can't help it. I want to know if Badger and Elvis are in the office or if they've already finished clearing it out, like Spinner told them to. I wonder why he needs a separate office from his grow-ops, anyway. He told Badger something about keeping good business records. Maybe having an actual office makes him feel like some sort of proper business dude. Man, that guy has some sort of strange and twisted view of himself.

The next building is a whole story higher, with no ladder to help me. I back up and sprint as hard as I can before I punch off. My sneakers bite into the brick and the brick bites into my fingers, but I do it. I grab hold of the roof edge and pull myself over the top. Across the other side, I peek carefully over the edge to the roof patio below and The Blue Turtle building at the other end of it. No sign of movement in the window. They must be finished and back at the warehouse.

I stand and jog to the edge, checking the street.

"What the...? Badger, it's the same kid!"

Elvis and Badger are standing beside the green Corvette, pointing up at me. Before I duck back out of sight, I see the trunk is open.

Oh, crud—what an idiot I am! I think fast and hard. It'll take them a little time to get to me...but I need that laptop. If I try to drop down now, they might get to me before I get to the bin—or just after, which is just as bad. I've got to draw them away!

I race along the front edge of the building, so that they can see me, and jump down to the roof one level below. I roll out and check the street. Good. They're following. I stay where they can see me. Ignoring their shouts, I leap the next space to the roof beyond. Let them think I'm a gazelle! Let them think I'm some sort of freaking superhero. They've probably seen parkour in the movies, though I doubt they'd have known what it was. They don't strike me as the kind of guys who are interested in healthy activities.

I'm not about to take the kind of risks stuntwomen take in the movies, but these guys don't know that. I pick up speed and wall-hop to the last roof, the one with three levels. Now I turn right, out of their line of sight. But before I do, I glance over my shoulder to see if they're keeping up.

They're out of shape so they're a little behind. At the back end of the building I check out the roof across the alley. It's the same level as the one I'm on, but it's too far away. The alley is narrow, but there's still no way I can jump it.

I don't have to.

chapter fourteen

Gathering all my breath, I let out an animal cry. I hope it sounds like triumph or maybe great effort. It doesn't matter. As long as they think I jumped. I turn and head back across the roofs I just came from, praying Badger and Elvis are as stupid as they look.

"Come on!" I hear Badger shout. "We'll get her at the next corner."

Yup. They're as stupid as they look.

Back on the roof nearest the Dumpster, I check the alley. Clear. I practically trip down the stairs—I'm going so fast—jump onto the Dumpster and down to the ground. I raise the lid and ignore the stench. Everything is as we left it. Whew!

I pull open the box, grab a handful of Sticklers and retrieve the laptop. Lowering the lid, I check the alley one more time. Still clear. Badger and Elvis aren't the brightest bulbs in the city, but it won't be long before they realize they've lost me. When that happens, they'll be back to check the alley and get the car.

I run out the other side of the alley, away from Badger and Elvis. At a government building three blocks away I find a sheltered space between two cement planters where I can sit and open the laptop.

Spinner gave us the answer. All I need to do is explore a few details.

With the laptop powered up, I open the Stickler program and click on all the maps available. Pretty soon I see a pattern. Besides the green warehouse and the office, there are five buildings that Spinner's thugs have made multiple trips to, and they are all in

The Exchange. Those have to be the other grow-ops! I memorize their locations, tuck the laptop back under my armpit and start running.

Five stops later, nearing the warehouse, I cross the construction zone. Rain sees me. She's already off the roof and coming to meet me.

"Plan B, then?" she asks.

"Plan B," I confirm. "Did you see anyone leave?"

"Badger and Elvis came back a few minutes ago. Cutter took Derek away. I haven't seen Billy or Spinner, but another guy I don't recognize just got here."

"That might be Cujo."

We cross the construction zone and head back along the main drag. At the corner two blocks up, we slow, turn north and blend with walking traffic. The next street over is the one with the warehouse. We turn onto it, watching carefully. I spot a pay phone just inside the doors of a basement café.

"Got a quarter?" I ask.

Rain shakes her head.

I bum a quarter off a guy coming out of the café. Now isn't the time to be proud.

I glance at my watch: 2:47. I go to pick up the phone, but Rain stops me.

"Let me talk," she says. "He might recognize your voice."

I nod and hand her the phone. Rain drops the coin in the slot, and I punch in Auntie Sylvia's number. I put my head close to Rain's so that I can hear too.

"Sylvia Gurniak's office," Spinner says. His voice is soft and singsong.

"Check your Stickler mobile lately?" Rain asks.

There's a pause.

"Who is this?"

"That doesn't matter. Just turn on your mobile," she says. Her face has gone pale. I hear his voice away from the phone. It's muffled, as if he's covering the phone with his hand and talking to someone.

"Okay, I've got it. I see you've been busy. What are you playing at, kid? What do you want?"

"The same thing everyone wants. Money."

Silence on the other end.

"As you can see, I know where your grow-ops are. You need to bring me some money, or I will sell the information to a rival gang."

"What about the laptop?"

Rain takes a deep breath. "You can have it back when you bring me the money. I want five thousand dollars."

"Where?"

"There's a wastebin by the labyrinth at the river park. Put the money inside and wait."

"What kind of steaming sack of bile is this? I give you the money, and I've got no guarantee you'll give me the laptop!"

"You have no choice."

"What time?"

"Um..." She looks at me and I shrug. "Five o'clock." She hangs up before Spinner can respond. As far as plans go, this one is full of holes. If we were really criminals, we'd have to be nuts to try something like this.

But we're not criminals. I'm not, anyway. Rain takes a deep breath and leans against the wall. She doesn't look like much of a criminal, either. Even good people have bad ideas sometimes. Maybe that's all it was.

The plan doesn't really matter. Not that one, anyway. I hold up crossed fingers in front of Rain. If Spinner reacts the way we think he will, he'll get his guys to move his grow-ops as quickly as possible. All of them.

Rain cups my hand in both of hers. "Don't worry. This will work."

"It has to."

Opening the door just a crack, we listen. Car tires squeal and motorcycles roar. Good! I power up the laptop and check the Stickler program.

"Looks good," Rain says. "Badger, Elvis, Cutter and Billy are all on the move. That means Derek's on his own. Cujo's still in the warehouse."

"We won't know where Spinner is," I point out. "He might go to Derek."

"He should be at the last grow-op. Six guys in total, six grow-ops. It makes sense."

"How's your ankle?" I ask.

"Sore, but I can manage."

I smile at her. I don't know if I could have handled all this on my own. "Okay," I say. "Let's rock and roll!"

I step into the stairwell and peek through the rails to the street. Normal daytime traffic. I can hear a siren, but it sounds far away.

City music.

We go the long way around the block toward the river, giving the warehouse a wide berth. The pump station is only a block away from the warehouse but next to the river. Outside of it, we halt.

The old, yellow, brick building looks still—no sign of activity, legal or otherwise. There's a metal grate attached to the front of a wooden door. It's padlocked. No way we can get through that way.

"This place used to be pretty important," Rain says. "It pumped water from the river through about eight miles of water lines to downtown fire hydrants."

"But they shut it down, right?"

"Uh-huh. Years ago."

"Good. If the ductwork is still in place, we might have our way in."

Tall, regally arched windows have had their glass replaced with gray-painted plywood. Not as pretty, perhaps, but less of a target for vandals. Tickle grass and wildflowers spill over the edges of moisture-rotted garden boxes. Soggy candy wrappers are ground into the dirt.

"There!" I say, grabbing hold of Rain's arm.

Halfway around the back of the building, butting up against the wall, a chain-link fence protects two more pieces of gray-painted plywood. These ones are laid flat on a raised platform. The base of the platform is concrete. I hand Rain the laptop; then I vault over the fence and land, palms flat on the wood. My landing sounds hollow, and I knock against the wood. Hopping sideways so my weight is off the wood, I dig my fingers between one edge of the wood and the concrete. It lifts! Only slightly, though. I can't get a good grip.

Rain has climbed over the fence to help.

"Try this," she says, reaching for a narrow length of steel that's resting on the ground beside the fence. She hands it to me and kneels beside me.

I wedge one end in the crevasse, and Rain and I lever the wood high enough to get our shoulders underneath. There is an open space under the wood, leading into the building. It's a section of culvert, and it's wide enough to crawl through. Leaving the plywood slightly off center, so light can filter in, I lower myself to the culvert and begin to crawl.

"Come on!" I call over my shoulder. "Hide the laptop in this entrance, and bring that steel bar in case we need it on the other end."

"Did I ever tell you I have a thing about small spaces?" Rain gasps.

"Just call this therapy then," I say. "I need you, Rain."

"I know."

Silently, we crawl. It feels like we're heading into Hell.

chapter fifteen

The dirt smell reminds me of digging up earthworms. The last time I did that was when Derek, Mom, Dad and I went camping in Northern Ontario three years ago. Dad was going to take me fishing. I dug up as many worms as I could find but when my sour cream container was full of squirming pink-and-gray worms, I was overwhelmed with guilt. They were such tiny, helpless creatures, and I was taking them away from their homes—from all they'd ever known. I returned them to the garden, and Dad and I went for a morning boat-ride instead.

Now, I'm the one crawling underground, except I'm also uprooted—me and Derek both are. There's something missing in Winnipeg, and I don't mean Mom and Dad. I've felt this way ever since we moved, even though Auntie Sylvia is trying hard to make us feel at home and loved.

In this dark place, looking for light, I have an idea. I think I know what's missing. It's Derek. Or rather, it's me and Derek together. We need to make things right between us. That's the only way Winnipeg will ever be home.

He has to be okay!

The grooved steel base of the culvert presses painfully into my knees. I feel like we're crawling downward, deeper into the earth. All around us there is the sound of water dripping, running and seeping. Finally, we tumble out the other end into a pit with a dirt floor.

There's light, but it's dim, glowing from some source I can't see. My eyes adjust quickly. I can see Rain blinking and looking around too. The pit has four concrete walls, with a metal ladder climbing up one side. Thank goodness! Not even parkour could help us up out of this—not enough space to take a run at it.

"We're sure he's here, right?" I whisper to Rain.

"No," Rain whispers back, "but I didn't hear any other plans, and the Stickler tracks showed Cutter coming here and then leaving after we called Spinner."

I want to call out, but I don't dare. It makes sense that Spinner has gone to the last grow-op, but we have no way of being sure. If Spinner *is* here, our only chance is to surprise him.

I strain to hear. All around, there is only the tinkle and drip of water.

Wait...was that a cough?

Yes, there it is again.

Stifling an urge to call out, I scramble up the ladder. Rain is right behind me. Peering up over the edge, I see the ceiling is much higher than it looked from outside. That means the inside is sunk below ground level. The dim light is bleeding down from old fluorescent tubes.

I can see machinery—there are giant gears and pulleys everywhere. Rain touches my shoulder and points to one giant red hook. It feels like we are tiny creatures wandering through the inner workings of some giant clock.

I search, dashing from gear to pulley. I hear another cough. It *has* to be Derek. But where is he?

Squinting into the gloom, I take note of dark open pits. I slow down and move more carefully, touching Rain's arm and pointing out the pits. I run my fingers gently along pieces of giant machinery. As long as I'm touching something—and as long as Rain is following me closely—I'm not as worried we will fall into someplace we shouldn't. We near one wall, and I blink.

We've found him! He's standing against some sort of support beam. No, he's hanging, his wrists tied to something above his head. He's not moving.

"Derek!" I say, as loud as I dare. I haven't seen or heard any sign of Spinner or anyone else in the building, but you never know. Derek doesn't move. "Derek!" I run to him and grab hold of him, hugging him. My eyes blur, and I blink away tears. We found him! He's alive!

"Nikki?" he croaks.

I let up on my hug and peer into his face. He's been badly beaten. It sounds like he can hardly speak, never mind shout. No wonder Spinner isn't worried about leaving him alone. I look up and see that his wrists are wrapped in chains.

"Rain, try that steel bar—hurry!"

"Try what with it? It's useless! We need chain cutters."

I glance around, looking for some sort of abandoned tool. How are we going to get him free? "We have to find something!" I cry.

"I'm on it," Rain says. She looks at Derek, swallows and squeezes my shoulder before leaving us.

As Rain scours the machinery around us, I hold Derek, trying to lift him a little and take some of the strain off his arms. I hear him sigh, and I hope it is with relief. "We'll get you free," I tell him.

"What are you doing here?" he whispers. His eyelids are swollen.

"We're here to get you out. Spinner is holding you hostage."

"I know that. What I don't know is why."

"Didn't they tell you anything?"

He shakes his head.

"It has to do with that court case Auntie Sylvia is working on."

"Gangs?"

"Yeah and police corruption. That's why we couldn't call the police." I touch his face. "But we had a plan, and the plan worked. As soon as we find a way to cut these chains, you'll be safe."

Rain grabs my arm. "I think someone's coming!" she hisses.

There's a scraping sound from the other side of the building. I look at Rain and see her panic; then I look back at Derek. He hears it as well. "Hide!" he rasps.

I don't want to go, but Rain pulls me

and we retrace our steps. On our hands and knees we crawl beneath some low vents close to the stairs. Close by there is something that looks like a huge piston with *DANGER* painted in red block letters on its side. No kidding. Any other time I might have found it funny.

Two lanky figures clatter down the steps above our heads and make their way toward Derek. One is wearing a denim jacket. Even without the powder-blue cap, I'd know him anywhere. It's Cujo. The other person has spiky blond hair and is wearing a duster. Spinner!

They have their backs to me and don't appear bothered by the dim lights. Of course, I think, anger flaming through me. They're rats, and rats like dark places. I calm my breathing. We have to stay very still. If we're caught now, we're all as good as dead.

The two men stand in front of Derek, as if waiting for him to speak. He lifts his head and looks surprised to see Cujo. But before he can say anything, Cujo drives his fist into his stomach. Derek brings his knees up, trying to protect himself.

I hold my own stomach and fight an impulse to scream.

chapter sixteen

"Why are you doing this?" Derek gasps. "What did I do to you?"

"You? Nothing, Derek," Cujo says. Gone is his cheery manner. "It's the damn judge."

"Auntie Sylvia? I don't understand."

"Shut up, Cujo," Spinner snaps.

"Why? It's not like it'll change anything. He should know what happens when people try and cross you, Spinner." He turns back to Derek. "She was warned months ago."

"What my aunt does has nothing to do with me," Derek wheezes.

"Maybe, maybe not," Cujo says. I feel goose-flesh rise on my arms as he begins to chuckle. "But thanks to you she's finally going to do the right thing—the right thing for us, anyway."

Spinner stands silent as Cujo paces back and forth, laughing.

"You want her to throw a case," Derek says.

"Always knew you were a smart kid. All we want is our guy," Cujo replies.

"For what? What good is he to you when everyone knows he's a bad cop?"

"We need him to be somewhere he can't talk, Derek. Spinner here has an empire to build."

"So what happens to me?" Derek asks. His voice is little more than a whisper. I watch, barely breathing.

Spinner steps in. "Isn't it obvious, Derek? You're going to throw yourself into that culvert over there and drown yourself."

Cujo jerks his head around, staring at Spinner, mouth open.

"Why would I do that?" Derek asks.

"Because you know too much."

"I won't tell."

"And I won't believe you," Spinner says.

"Wait," Cujo says, stepping in. "He's just a kid. I didn't sign on for murder."

"You didn't sign on for the chess club either, Cujo."

"But I—"

"Enough!" Spinner snaps. "Open the gate."

Cujo turns to Spinner, as if he might challenge him. Instead he shrugs and walks to some nearby machinery. I hear a clank of metal and a creak. Cujo twists his body as if he's turning a giant wheel. As the sound of rushing water fills my ears, I see Spinner go to Derek. He reaches up and unlocks the chains holding his wrists. Derek crumples to the ground.

Cujo returns and picks up something from the ground. The metal bar! Rain must have dropped it when she was searching for a better tool.

"What are you going to do with that,

Cujo?" Spinner shouts. The sound of rushing water must be louder where he is. I can hear him clearly, but maybe he can't hear himself.

"Nothing," Cujo shouts back. He looks back and forth between Derek and Spinner, as if he's trying to work something out. "I'm still wondering why we have to kill the kid. We're getting our stuff back, and the aunt is in your pocket. No one will say anything."

"We are going to kill the kid, Cujo, because we need to show we are strong."

"I don't understand."

Spinner shakes his head. "Cujo, Cujo, Cujo. Maybe you're not as tough as your name makes you sound. Maybe you're just a puny, piddling, puppy dog."

"No," Cujo says, "I did everything you told me to. I stood in front of that building for three months and made these people think I was their friend."

"Are you?"

"Am I what?"

"Their friend? I need strong men on my team, Cujo. Not puppy dogs."

Cujo glances at Derek and then squares himself, facing Spinner. "I'm strong," he says. "I can do this."

"Good," Spinner says. "Prove it, and you're in for double what you were before."

"I am?"

"Oh yes. Not only that, but I'll make you my number one guy."

"I thought that was Billy."

"Billy's a punk, Cujo. A guy like you who stands around for three months pretending he's someone he's not has potential. I can use a guy like you. Could be worth a lot of money to you."

"Good," Cujo says. "That's what I want."

He turns back to Derek and kicks him in the belly.

I clap my hand over my mouth as Cujo moves to kick him again. But this time Derek doesn't cry out. I see dirt fly. Did Cujo miss? I don't see how he could, but then it dawns on me. Did he miss on purpose?

I glance at Spinner. From his angle, it must look like the kicks are connecting.

Cujo kicks again and again without connecting. Derek starts crying out with every kick, even though he's not being hurt. He must realize what Cujo's doing—or not doing.

Maybe Cujo is just another guy who had a bad idea. Maybe he's sorry about that now and is trying to help. Or maybe he has a plan of his own. Whatever. At least Derek is being spared the pain.

"Finish him off, Cujo," Spinner says.

"What—now?" Cujo asks, panting a little.

"Take that metal bar and hit him in the head. An unconscious boy will drown much faster."

Cujo stares at him a minute. Then he looks at the metal bar. "Right," he says. He turns back to Derek and winds up to hit him.

I hold my breath.

Cujo's arm falls with mighty force, but I can see that he hasn't hit Derek. He's hit his own leg! It must hurt like hell, but he doesn't let on.

My eyes blur with relief. Cujo isn't a murderer.

Derek must be playing dead. He's not

moving. Cujo grabs him and yanks him toward the culvert. Before I can process what's happening, he's hoisted Derek over the edge.

"No!" I cry, but I slap my hand over my mouth before it gets all the way out. Rain and I exchange a worried look. I freeze as they turn to leave and walk close to where we're hidden. On the first stair, Spinner stops and faces Cujo.

"This is where you and I finish," he says, his voice steady as stone.

They're close enough that I can see the confusion in Cujo's eyes.

"But I'm going to be your number one... what do you mean?"

"I mean you talk too much."

"What—the kid? He's gone. Not a problem."

I open my eyes wide, mirroring Cujo's, as Spinner pulls something from inside his duster.

In gloved hands, he's holding a knife. Before Cujo can react with anything more than shock, Spinner closes the gap between them. He plunges the knife into Cujo's ribs, and Cujo crumples onto the ground. Spinner steps away, leaving the knife where he's stuck it.

chapter seventeen

I cover my mouth and nose, trying to stifle a scream. Rain is gripping my arm so hard, it's numb. I can't stop the hiccupy sobs that come next even though I'm terrified Spinner might hear.

Spinner looks completely focused on Cujo.

"You understand, Cujo," he says, his voice harsh. "It's important that I show I'm strong." He turns and strides up the metal stairs toward the door. As soon as I hear the clank of the door shutting, Rain and I crawl from our hiding place. As I rush to where Derek disappeared, I see Rain stop to check on Cujo.

"Derek!" I yell, no longer caring if I'm heard. "Derek!" I grasp the edges of the culvert and look down. I see him! There's water sloshing below him, but somehow he's stopped his fall. Unlike the culvert Rain and I crawled through, this one runs vertically. Derek is angled across the opening. His feet are anchored on one side and his hands are on the other.

"Derek!" I yell again, reaching for him, but he's too far down. How far down is he?

"Cujo's dead, Nikki," Rain says, joining me.

I nod. There's nothing we can do for him. I'll be sick about it later, but for now we need to focus on Derek. "Tell me you're okay!" I call to him.

Slowly, Derek cranks his head to the side and glances up at me. It must be hard for him, because he looks down again. "Hi, Nikki," he says. His voice is calm. "Hi Nikki's friend."

I can hear him clearly, and I notice the water is no longer rushing. Wherever it came from, it must have found someplace else to go.

"We'll get help!" I cry.

For a moment, he doesn't respond. "There's no time," he says finally.

"What do you mean?"

"The water's rising, Nikki. I can't hang on."

I stare at the water. It's black against the grooved metal of the culvert. I don't know if it's rising, but it is moving—that much I can see. "Of course you can."

"I'm telling you, by the time you get help I'll be swimming, and the way I feel, I won't be swimming for long."

I look harder at the water. He's right. It is rising. Not fast—but definitely rising. I see a run-off gap just above his head—his hands are wrapped around the edge of it. The water will rise no higher. That means there's no way he can just float to the top.

"Then you have to climb out."

"I can't." He's gasping and grunting. It

must be taking every bit of strength he has left just to hold on.

"You have to!"

This time when he speaks, I have to strain to hear. "It's better this way," he says.

Shock jolts through me. It's as if I've been stabbed, just like Cujo. This isn't about his not being able to hang on. It's about his not wanting to.

"You can't give up, Derek!"

"Just let it go, Nikki."

"No...no I won't! Cujo is dead because he tried to give you a chance. If he'd really hit you, you'd be dead right now. Rain and I could have been killed too. Don't you care about that?"

He doesn't say anything—just keeps staring down at the dark water.

"Derek...you can't give up! I need you."

"We've been through this, Nikki." He stops, and I can hear him panting, trying to catch his breath. "You needed Mom and Dad," he gasps. "I should have died in that fire, not them."

Suddenly I feel anger spark and build—like the terrible fire that took Mom and Dad. "No!" I roar. It's as if I'm shouting with all the pain and resentment I've been hiding since that horrible night. "You can't do this! You can't leave me too!"

Derek twists his head to look at me again. I can see the anguish in his eyes. Maybe he sees it in mine too.

"It's my fault they're gone, Nikki. I know you hate me."

Tears blur my vision. "I don't hate you, Derek. You're my brother. I love you."

"But it's my fault."

"No...no it's not." I swallow, hard. "I did blame you. But I don't anymore. I can't."

As soon as I say it, I know it's true. I also know that Mom and Dad are here with us, right now. I feel myself letting go of my anger, and it's okay.

"It was an accident, Derek. A terrible tragic accident."

He looks away, back down below. I can hear him sniffling.

"You always told me that the good thing

about falling down is getting up again, Derek. I need you to get up!"

"I..."

"Get up, Derek!" I scream. Tears are falling freely now, and I scream again. "Get up! Get up!"

"Nikki!"

It must have taken a lot of effort for him to raise his voice, but I hear him. Barely. I shake my head and wipe my eyes. I feel weak. "Derek...please don't leave me. If you die, it'll kill me too. Can't you see?"

He looks down and then up again. After a moment, he speaks. "I don't know if I can do this..."

"You can." Hope. I feel hope. It's so strong I think it might knock me over. "You can do this, Derek. It's just like parkour."

"What?"

"You climbed that space at the zoo. Remember?"

He was the best of his parkour team and the strongest. That day he had been showing off a little. He'd planted his feet on one side of the curved concrete hall in the monkey house and his hands on the other. Bit by bit he'd inched his way up. I watched his arms and legs shake and knew it must be taking all his strength. He's lost some of that strength since then, but the culvert is grooved. That has to make it easier.

He nods and then lifts one hand, then the other, one foot, then the other. Slowly, grunting with every move, he climbs. As he gets closer, I can see his whole body shaking. A little closer, and Rain and I grab hold of him. We heave backward and pull him free. I fall with him to the floor and hold him, sobbing. It's all I can do.

Maybe he would have died in the culvert, and maybe he wouldn't have. But climbing out means he's choosing life. My big brother is back.

After a moment, Derek looks up and turns his head toward Cujo. "Did you say he's dead?"

I nod.

Groaning, he pulls himself up and limps over to Cujo. He sits beside him, fingers to his neck. Rain and I join him.

I look at Cujo's face. All I want to do is run screaming from the room, but I wait. I wait for my brother.

Cujo's eyes flutter and then open.

He's alive? I jump up, grabbing Rain.

Cujo looks at Derek. "Good," he whispers. His breath comes in wheezy gasps. "I didn't want you dead." He rasps. "I was just..."

"I know," Derek says. "Thank you."

Cujo gives one weak nod and then closes his eyes again.

"We've got to get help," Derek says.

chapter eighteen

"I thought he was dead!" Rain cries.

"I'll stay with him," Derek says. "Move!"

Rain and I emerge from the building as if being birthed. The light is too bright. There's a lot of noise...sirens. An ambulance screeches to a halt on the street in front of us, followed by two police cars. Rain runs to the ambulance.

My knees buckle, and all I can do is sit on the ground and watch. I think I'm crying. I touch my cheeks. Yes, definitely crying. But it's like I'm not really here.

A moment later two guys jump from the ambulance, bags in hand, and follow Rain into the pump station. From one of the police cars, a familiar figure emerges. That brings me back.

"Angel!"

He shuffles over, his eyes full of concern. "I told you I know some people," he says.

I throw my arms around him, not caring anymore if I scare him. "You really are my angel," I cry, tears dampening his grizzled whiskers.

He hugs me back and then he steps away, nodding, as if he's embarrassed. Before I can say anything else, someone else is grabbing me and hugging me tight.

"Auntie Sylvia!"

"Oh, Nik! What an awful day...but everything's okay now."

I think of Cujo. "Not everything," I say. "Besides, I had some help." I smile at Angel and take Rain by the hand as she joins us. "These are my friends, Rain and Angel."

"Nice to meet you, Ms...I mean Your Honorable...um. I'm sorry, what do I call a judge?" Rain blushes.

Auntie Sylvia laughs. "If you're in my courtroom you call me 'My Lady,'" she says, winking. "But Ms. Gurniak is fine."

I look at Rain and smile. "You're not planning on seeing Auntie Sylvia in court, are you, Rain?"

Rain jabs me with her elbow. "No!"

"Sure?"

"Really," she says, watching as two ambulance attendants emerge from the pump station, carrying Cujo on a stretcher. "This is as close as I ever want to get to this kind of thing." She turns to me. "And never again, agreed?"

"Agreed!" I say. "Did they catch Spinner, Auntie Sylvia?"

Auntie Sylvia shakes her head and nods toward the police officer who looks like he's in charge. He's busy talking to Derek. "According to Sergeant Popowich over there, they already knew about Spinner and his grow-ops. They just didn't know where they were hidden."

"The laptop! We hid it in the back. It shows where the grow-ops are."

"They can also track Spinner's guys with it," Rain says, grinning. "I'll go get it!"

Auntie Sylvia squeezes my hand. "Don't worry. Sergeant Popowich is a good man. Spinner won't be free for long."

"Cujo was in on it, you know," I say, feeling another lump build in my throat. "But he tried to help Derek."

We watch as another police car arrives and two more officers enter the pump station. I see movement out of the corner of my eye. It's Angel. The police must not need him right now, or maybe they've already finished, because he's leaving. It looks like he might be heading back to his favorite bench by the river.

"I want to talk to Angel for a minute, Auntie Sylvia. Can I?"

Auntie Sylvia nods. "Yes, but be quick. Sergeant Popowich needs to speak with each of you."

I look over at Sergeant Popowich, who is opening the laptop and listening intently to

Rain. I jog to catch up with Angel and find him around the corner on the sidewalk that meanders alongside the river. He glances at me and nods, like he always does. This time, though, I see a smile and some crinkling around his eyes.

"I just wanted to say thanks."

"Your hug was thanks enough," he says. "Haven't been hugged in a long time."

This makes me wonder. "You said you used to be a police officer, Angel."

"That's right."

"What happened? Did you retire?"

"That's right," he says again.

I look at him. With his whiskers and rumpled clothes, I never imagined him as someone who'd had a regular job or a history of any kind. I wouldn't make that mistake again.

"I thought that when people retire they like to sit on beach chairs somewhere, sipping drinks with umbrellas."

He flashes a grin at me. "That's not me," he says. "I like downtown. I live here. I watch things."

Looking forward again, he starts humming, as if that's the end of our conversation. Maybe it is—for now.

I see that we've already passed the street the warehouse is on. We've also gone past an old furniture factory with a fading mural still stamped on its side. There are two new buildings being constructed beside it. Probably more condos. A flash of red near the farthest building catches my eye.

"Spinner!" I cry, grabbing Angel's sleeve and stopping him.

Spinner's in his red T-shirt—that was what caught my attention. He must have dropped his coat somewhere.

"That guy?" Angel asks. "I know him. He's bad news."

"We've got to get the police!" I watch as Spinner disappears inside a network of steel beams and lumber. I realize that in a few minutes he'll be gone.

"Angel," I say, turning to him. "I'll follow him and see where he's going. You get the police, okay?"

He nods. "Be careful."

"Always."

I sprint across the street and into the new building. I see a flash of red at the end of a lengthy corridor and follow it. Does he know the way through? I hope so. I'd rather chase him on a wide-open street than in a building.

There he is! A flash of daylight tells me he's found his way out. I follow and pound the pavement behind him. He runs pretty fast for an old guy!

I zig, and he zags. Soon we're running through a maze of back alleys I've never explored. We're close to the train bridge. The sounds of banging and clacking and roaring freight overwhelms and blocks out the normal downtown sounds.

"What the...?" I stop, puffing slightly. It's a dead-end! Where'd he go?

I hear a voice shouting above the train noise. "You looking for me, kid?"

I whirl around. "Spinner!"

"I don't think we've met. At least...not in person."

I vault over a trashcan, flinging it behind

me and running deeper into the dead-end. At the end I tic-tac off a brick wall, pivot 180 degrees and grasp a hanging stair. Spinner is right there, reaching for me! I swing my legs from back to front for momentum and fling myself forward, avoiding his clutch. Letting go of the stair, I land in the alley beyond him. I hear him curse. It distracts me, and I land wrong. One knee hits where it shouldn't have, and I cry out. I grit my teeth. If there was ever a time to cowgirl up, this is it. Hauling myself back up to standing, I run for all I'm worth.

I turn left at the corner and am back on the street. Where are all the people? This is downtown, for god's sake. There are supposed to be shoppers!

"Help!" I yell. "Someone!"

"Give it up." I hear him huff. "I saw you on camera. You're mine now!"

"Not yet I'm not—not ever!"

The trains are moving off to their next connection, taking their creaking and rumbling with them. I can almost feel Spinner's hot breath on my neck. His rasps and gasps tell me he's right on my heels. As I look for an escape, I spot someone else running directly toward me. Finally! Wait. They don't know what they're running into! What if Spinner has another knife?

"Get out of the way!" I scream. "He's dangerous."

As the running man approaches and passes me, I have a sense of him rising up and leaping. I twist my head sideways in time to see him grab hold of a rail that might have once held a hanging sign. With all the built-up speed of his run, he thrusts his legs forward like a battering ram.

Spinner doesn't see it coming. He's knocked flat. Out cold.

The running man turns. It's the guy with the wolf eyes!

"Hello, Karma," he says.

chapter nineteen

It's another hot day in Winnipeg. Earlier, a storm ripped through the city, soaking everything and cooling it a bit, but that brief relief is no match for the August sun.

I spot T-mac waiting for Derek and me underneath the bridge, warming up. Others might prefer to cool down.

"Hey, T-mac!" I call, waving. "Fancy running into you here."

T-mac smiles. It's been our joke ever since he'd slammed his size thirteens into Spinner's

Anita Daher

belly. When I'd smashed into him on his bicycle that day, and then he returned the favor coming out of the bookstore, I'd never have guessed that he would end up saving me.

And he's a traceur! I wouldn't have guessed that, either.

All T-mac had known was that some creep was chasing a girl, and he thought he'd better help out. He helped all right. When Spinner's head hit the pavement, he was not only knocked unconscious, but he ended up in the hospital in a coma.

Using the files on the laptop, the police were able to figure out the details of Spinner's plan, and they rounded up everyone involved—including the remaining corrupt officers on the force. Meanwhile, Spinner slumbered away happily in his coma. He wasn't very happy when he woke up three days later. Some people think the number three is lucky. Not Spinner.

Cujo is still in the hospital, but it looks like he'll recover. Derek has been visiting him when Sergeant Popowich lets him. Derek says

160

Cujo is cooperating with police. He'll still go to jail, though. No avoiding that.

Hard to believe all that went down only two weeks ago. So many lives have been changed! Some for the better. Like mine. Today is my sixteenth birthday. This morning Derek gave me a book about David Belle and Sébastien Foucan, two of the original traceurs, the ones responsible for bringing parkour to the world.

Derek's life is better too. It's like he's woken up from a nightmare and he's finally got his eyes wide open. He's a traceur again. And I'm a traceuse. I smile, remembering my race away from Badger and Elvis. Thanks to those two idiots I learned that I can even leap rooftops. If I need to, anyway. Roof-jumping isn't something any traceuse or traceur does on a normal day. Too dangerous.

"Are you ready to run, Karma?" T-mac asks. I smile. As far as nicknames go, this one pretty much rocks. Just like T-mac, I decide. He turns to Derek. "Glad you could join us, Aqua."

"Aqua?"

"If the pump station fits...," T-mac says, winking. Derek grins and shrugs.

We jog with T-mac toward the Oodena Celebration Circle at The Forks, where we're to meet up with the rest of the guys from Winnipeg Parkour. The Circle was built in honor of the aboriginal people who first lived here. It symbolizes their traditional meeting place and the heart of the city. It is also a great place to warm up for parkour.

Turns out that when I told Rain there were no parkour teams in Winnipeg, I was wrong. I just wasn't looking in the right place.

"Wait for me!"

Speak of the devil. Rain is running to join us.

"I just got off work," she explains.

I smile. Rain got a job at an electronics store at The Forks shopping mall. She's thrilled to be able to mess with all her favorite tech stuff and even more thrilled to be making some money. I'm just happy it's honest money.

"It's okay," I say. "You're just in time."

We wave hello to Hawk, Zeddy and the rest of the gathering gang. Zeddy is walking on his hands again. Man, that guy could live in an upside-down world, if he wants to. Then again, maybe this world is upside down enough.

As Rain and I warm up on the grass, I see Derek laugh at something T-mac says. Then he runs toward a rounded column—part of the Oodena Celebration Circle. It's concrete, inlaid with river stone, and about twenty feet high, as are the other columns in the circle. In a blink he's three steps up the side of it and into a perfect wall-flip. It sure didn't take him long to get back in shape.

"So, when are you going?" Rain asks.

I look at her, loving that my friend's cat eyes are full of concern for me. Rain knows I can handle what's coming. She makes me believe it too.

"We leave tomorrow on the six-AM flight."

"Early!"

"Yeah. Auntie Sylvia thought that would be best. We'll go to the cemetery first and

163

then see some friends. After that, if we feel up to it, we'll go to the house."

"Will you?"

"Feel up to it? Probably not, but I think we have to see it. I do, anyway. I think it's important."

Rain pokes her chin toward Derek, who is leaping from the top of one concrete column to another. Hawk and Zeddy are following him, as T-mac and the others watch from below. "Is he going to be okay?"

I sigh. "Yeah, I think so. He needed me to forgive him before he could forgive himself. But I couldn't forgive him until I admitted that I blamed him. It was one big circle, you know?"

"Have you forgiven him?"

"Absolutely. It really wasn't his fault."

"It was that girl's fault."

I shake my head. "I can't think that way, Rain. It doesn't help."

I'll miss Mom and Dad forever. Derek will too. But blaming someone and staying angry is a trap. It holds me down, and I want more than anything to feel free.

Parkour is about going over or through any obstacle in my path. It's about making it a part of my journey, not a roadblock.

I like the Winnipeg Parkour team a lot. Unlike The Rude Boyz, this team welcomed me just because I want to run. Derek and Rain were welcomed for the same reason. It has nothing to do with being old enough or good enough.

But it *helps* that I'm good!

There's a shout from the sidewalk at the edge of the circle. "Help him!" a woman cries. She's just watched Zeddy drop from the top of the concrete column and tumble down the slope below.

"He's okay!" Derek shouts from above. "He meant to do that!"

"You kids get out of here!" the woman says, shaking her fist. Wait a minute...the woman looks familiar. It's Jane Jogger! Joe Jogger appears, handing her an ice-cream treat. He must have bought it from one of those bicycle carts. I can hear the telltale tinkle-bell from somewhere over the hill.

"You can't go around scaring people like that," Joe Jogger scolds. "Why don't you go play on a skateboard or something?"

Rain and I laugh. We leap to our feet, ready to join Derek, T-mac and the others in a run. We follow the path, vaulting over benches and precisioning from post to post to post. Hawk looks like he wants to turn off before the bridge and head downtown.

"Not yet!" I call. "Have you ever been to the labyrinth?"

Hawk shakes his head. "Lead the way!"

And so I do—under the bridge and through the park, along the curve of the river. On the way we pass Dog Guy. Today he has two golden Labs and something that looks like a pot-scrubber with legs. He also has the same old Saint Bernard, which looks like he wants to run with us. It's all Dog Guy can do to hang on.

Angel is sitting on his bench in front of the labyrinth.

"Hello, Angel!" I call.

"Hello, Nikki," he calls back. Some of

the others on my team also greet him. I'm not sure if they know him or are just being friendly. Maybe both.

"Hey, Angel."

"How's it goin', Angel?"

Some nicknames just fit.

I leap onto one of the walls of the labyrinth and drink in the shouts and laughter of the others as they climb and leap up, down and all over the structure. They're discovering it. Feeling it out. Just like I did at first.

In the space between where my sneakers leave the concrete and where they hit the top of the next wall, I feel free. The concrete walls of Winnipeg's River Park Labyrinth are mine. I *own* them.

It feels like flying.

Anita Daher began her life in a small town on Prince Edward Island but left at the age of five, remaining something of a gypsy ever since. Her writing reflects the places she's been blessed to spend time. Her most recent Orca book is *Racing for Diamonds*. Anita lives in Winnipeg, Manitoba, with her husband, two daughters, one basset hound and a Westfalia camper van named Mae.